NORTHLIGHT, LOVELIGHT

People do not realize how much time and effort it costs to learn to read. I have labored 80 years to that end, but cannot say that I have yet succeeded.

JOHANN WOLFGANG VON GOETHE

Everything in this world exists only to take its place in a book.

STÉPHANE MALLARMÉ

NORTHLIGHT, LOVELIGHT

Jacques Folch-Ribas

Fitzhenry & Whiteside
Toronto Montreal Winnipeg Vancouver

First published in the French language as
"Une aurore boréale"
© Éditions Robert Laffont, S.A., 1974

English translation copyright © 1976 by Reader's Digest Association,
Inc.

Manufactured in the United States of America

Translated by Jeremy J. Leggatt

Library of Congress Cataloging in Publication Data

Folch-Ribas, Jacques E
    Northlight, lovelight.

    Translation of Une aurore boréale.
    I. Title.
PZ4.F656No3   [PQ2666.03]   843'.9'14   76–20521

ISBN 0–88349–106–0

10 9 8 7 6 5 4 3 2 1

Once there was a man whose name was Pierre, but everyone called him Le Rouge. Perhaps it was his red hair and fair skin that had earned him this nickname. The few people who had met him said he was half Indian. Perhaps because his face was hairless. Perhaps it was because he lived alone, a hermit life in a rough log cabin between the forest and the gulf. Or perhaps it was because of his known skills at hunting and fishing. These people, the people who knew him, also said he was mad; they said he talked to himself, that he ate raw meat. Perhaps loneliness had done this to him. If these are oversimplifications, it's because the people of Baie-des-Epaulards—a place of rocks, sand, woods, and one poor village that the maps call Orcs Bay—are by nature careless of facts.

Although nobody really knew where this Pierre had come from, people casually accepted and passed on a story put together bit by bit over the years. Long ago, the story went, a white man had come from far away, perhaps from the south. He had a very young woman with him, who looked like an Indian. They had built a cabin on the shore, its back to a small forest which was almost at the end of the bay. Some people said the cabin had been there as long as anyone could remember, and that the couple had merely moved in and made it habitable again. They had lived there a long time, keeping to themselves, almost never going to the village. And one day Pierre was born. That is what they said at Orcs Bay.

In this place the North American continent ends in a mountainous peninsula, an almost uninhabited crescent covered with forests and swampy *savanes*— wet, uncertain zones of tall grass and scrawny trees. A whole country could sprawl there—cities, highways, long prosperous valleys, a thousand small white villages, and along its steep coastline a thousand coves and a thousand beaches that would take a lifetime to explore. But it is not so. This is the very end of the world, scarcely touched by man, and there is almost nothing here but nature: forests, endless and unchanging, broken only by lakes teeming with birds and by mountain streams disintegrating into rock-strewn rapids; bare slopes of upland prairies swept by scorching summer winds and whistling winter blizzards; a few small towns, a few clapboard villages, a few poor farms; here and there a stubby jetty piled high with logs waiting for the towboat. A road links all

2

this together, winding and unwinding like an interminable length of rope, beginning and ending who knows where.

At the farthest point, at the very edge of this extreme land, the gulf curves sharply eastward and the opposite shore fades out of sight even with its lofty mountains. Here a succession of small bays looks across the water toward the Iles-aux-Ours. This is Bas-du-Fleuve, the land where the suns set in flames. And here, abandoned to the open water of the gulf, isolated from the mainland by an almost impassable mountain crest, is Baie-des-Epaulards. The road makes its appearance here surreptitiously, a ribbon of earth and gravel that snakes across wooded slopes toward the fishermen's houses, that slithers past the church, and then suddenly pulls up, mindless and befuddled, at the wall of the cemetery by the water's edge.

The bay people also say that Le Rouge's parents had both died on the same day somewhere on the gulf. Perhaps as they tracked a fur seal over by the Iles-aux-Ours. They must have fallen through the thin, aging ice, just before the springtime rout.

They would go out together across the frozen bay every year, but they had always refused to take Pierre. "It is too dangerous; three people would be too heavy," his mother would say. "And the country on the other side is immense. It has no end." They would pack their sled with provisions—salt, guns, and clothing—leaving Pierre a rifle and everything he needed for the few days they would be away. Then they would leave, with the dog. When they came back, the sled would be full of pelts, meat, and frozen fish.

But that time his parents did not return. The days passed, and from time to time Pierre would stand on the edge of a chaos of broken and jagged ice, staring into the distance until his eyes hurt and he could no longer see anything. Then he would go back to the cabin, frozen and numb, make himself some soup, and go to bed. The next day he would watch again.

It was a traveling peddler who rescued him from this half-waking state—a man they called the Voyageur, who called at the cabin once or twice each winter when he was passing through the bay. Pierre heard the horn of his truck coming from the far side of the forest. He got out of bed and left the cabin. The peddler, surprised that no one had come to meet him, finally appeared through the trees. He asked Pierre some question, then nodded thoughtfully: "Perhaps they'll be back. How many days did you say? You don't remember. Hmmm... No, they won't be back. They'd never make it. It's impossible. The ice is breaking up all the time. They'd be mad to try crossing! I'll take a look around the cabin. I'll let you know what you need and sell it to you. Do you have money? Or pelts, like your father? Shall we take a look?" He paused, as if sizing up Pierre, then nodded again. "You're big enough to get by—you're a man! Let's see now, let's take a look...." The Voyageur took some pelts and left ammunition and feed.

No one ever saw Pierre's parents again. No one knew. It had all happened so long ago. But what had happened?

4

The gulf is treacherous. The bay is deceitful. And Bas-du-Fleuve, with its waters that are neither salt nor fresh, is an uncertain place.

At times it is truly a river, swollen out of all proportion, flushing monstrous volumes of fresh water and ice out to sea. At such times you cannot see the far shore through the rain and the falling snow. You can only make out the dim green shadow of the Iles-aux-Ours, half-drowned under the dingy white sky. Little by little the ice stops moving and hardens into strange shelving shapes, huge chaotically welded blocks stretching as far as the eye can see and crisscrossed by a thousand slow-moving streams. And for many years now, since that day when the Voyageur said, "No, they won't be back. They'd never make it," Pierre leaves his cabin at this time of the year to hunt along the shores of the bay, tracking Arctic hare, fox, muskrat, and marmot. Sometimes he hunts further afield, on the ice, occasionally even venturing out to the Iles, four hours' hard walking away. From the Iles you can see the black wall of the far shore, the land without an end. The land of Pierre's mother Nod.

At other times the gulf is a sea. It is hot and the wind never stops blowing. Deep waves, stained tawny under the summer sun, roll in to assault the land. Or else the slack of calm days leaves the sea like a flat mirror where white porpoise bellies flash in the heat and the haze. The air smells of salt and seaweed, and Pierre goes down to inspect his catch. Twice a day, at low tide, he walks down to the narrow, still-submerged gullet of his fascine dam and methodically empties it. There are herring, sardine, sometimes a sturgeon, and often slimy gray sea slugs. Clouds of gulls mill frantically around him, showering him with squawks and droppings.

Season flowed imperceptibly into season for Pierre. It was a long time, several years in fact, since he had even thought about the people in the village, those people whose existence had once intrigued him. News of the outside world came to him over a tiny radio— the Voyageur replaced its batteries for him—so that Pierre knew many things. He understood some of them and was very curious about others. But he had no wish to go and find out about them because people frightened him a little. It was a dull, indistinct fear, like his fear of everything he did not understand. His one visit to the village on the bay had only added to his fear.

That one time when he had left his hermit's lair was because of his rifle. It had happened many years ago, but he remembered it well. The Voyageur could not repair guns. ("I could bring you a new one, but it would cost too much.") He had looked through his truck, but he had no part like the hammer Pierre had showed him. "If you like, Le Rouge," he went on, "I'll take you over to the village and bring you back this evening. I'm in a good mood today, so take advantage of the ride. You can just give me a marten pelt." He had laughed, as well. Pierre needed the rifle, even though he used it rarely and never missed a shot. And the mysterious village of Orcs Bay intrigued him. So he had agreed to go.

After the rough track on the forest rim you reach the dirt road which cuts across the *savane* with its

6

blackened, wind-tortured, emaciated pines. Pierre crouched tensely in the front seat, seeing the pines go by but no longer recognizing them. And he watched the Voyageur's hands twisting and turning the iron bar that ended in a black mound between his feet and Pierre's. The truck made an infernal noise as it jolted along, swerving ceaselessly to the right and to the left. After many detours, after crossing a dismal cement bridge and a wide grassland where dirty sheep were grazing, they reached the village. There was a long street; it seemed crowded to Pierre. They stopped in front of a brightly colored store, and the Voyageur led Pierre up to a long counter. An old man took the rifle, examined it, and vanished behind a door. Pierre looked at everything. There were many things there, some of them unknown to him, and everything had a terrible odor—sour, indeterminate smells that irritated his throat. The old man came back with the rifle, and Pierre checked the hammer. It was good and well made. He paid what he was told to pay.

Then the Voyageur told him he should wait. He would be back in the afternoon. "You can eat across the way if you're hungry. They'll sell you whatever you want. . . . Yes, it's him all right, it's Le Rouge," he added to some men who had come into the store. And he left.

Pierre went out, cradling the rifle. People were watching him. He walked a little way, but thought it would be better not to get too far from the store in case he couldn't find it again. He looked carefully in every direction. Too many things looked alike, and there were too many of them: Pierre's senses were beginning to reel. Children ran up and milled around him. He said a few words, but they laughed, shouted insults, stuck out their tongues, and then fled, frightened perhaps by their own daring, or by the rifle. A woman in blue came out of a doorway, picked out one of the children, slapped him, and drove him yelling back into the house.

Pierre walked a little farther, then sat down on the grass. But soon he noticed an old man under a wooden porch, smoking and staring at him. Pierre got up and moved again. He looked for trees, for cover, but there was nothing nearby. A car drew up beside him. The policeman looked out, recognized him, nodded, turned back to the steering wheel and drove off without saying a word.

Pierre walked on, looking at everything as he went. He reached what seemed to be the end of that long street and came to fields bordered by fences of silvered wood. He stopped, and sat down with his back to a post. Suddenly the village no longer interested him; time dragged on endlessly. Then, afraid of being left behind, he headed back in the direction of the store.

At last the Voyageur appeared. Without getting out, he opened the truck door for Pierre and they bounced away. The Voyageur was singing; he was drunk, he laughed a lot, and smelled of beer. He waited at the end of the truck near the cabin while Pierre went to get the marten pelt.

That was all Pierre knew of the village. That night he hardly slept because of everything he had seen, and because of a tension that faded only very gradually. By morning, however, when the crows and ravens were beginning to call and the sun had reached the base of the trees, it had vanished.

That had been some years ago. Pierre remembered it all, and the village on the bay no longer aroused his curiosity. It was nothing like the outside world he had pictured as he listened to his radio. But his old, vague sense of mystery continued, now becoming more defined into a powerful need, the need to meet someone, a someone he imagined and talked to. In autumn and winter Pierre didn't think about it much. His chores, his hunting, and the need to survive took up all his time. But with the dawning of spring the need to talk to that someone and the need to meet that someone were reborn in him.

It was at this time of the year that Pierre set up his fascine dam, and at every low tide he splashed down to the narrow lower tip of the pen and pulled out fish.

As the tide came back in, he went into the forest to lay traps and snares, bending down branches the way his father had taught him, so that when an animal was caught the branch would spring back up and hold the game high in the air, out of reach. Or else he crouched in one of his hides. He seldom needed the rifle. He could kill anything that came near with a club, a knife, and particularly with a long whip—another trick his father had taught him.

Then he packed his fish, the previous day's game, pelts if he had any, and whatever else that seemed marketable, into a birch-bark sack. This he hung from his shoulder, and went off to find the summer visitors. The villagers of Baie-des-Epaulards no longer interested him. But strangers, outsiders from the world the radio spoke of, did.

Far from the tangled woods where Pierre nested, beyond the prairie and the slimy, seaweed-strewn mud flats of the shore, a tree-covered promontory of rock and mud thrusts out into the sea. People call it the Cape. A road runs along this headland between big frame houses half hidden by trees. In winter the Cape is dead, and almost inaccessible under deep snow. In spring the houses open one after another as the vacationers arrive. Some come in gleaming cars, others in old jalopies. Children shout, play, and cry. Chimneys smoke day and night. People go up and down all day long, visiting each other or driving down to the village for provisions. Men with complicated lines fish along the water's edge. Sometimes a motorboat roams the gulf. Women hang out washing on lines slung between trees. People saw wood, hammer, fix their houses. But all this teeming activity down on the ground is hidden from view by clusters of tall pines that shelter crows and herring gulls in their tops.

Pierre would walk down the Cape road, hoping to be noticed as he went past the houses. He never walked onto someone's property, even if it was unprotected by hedges or fences. If no one called out to him, he would walk by a little sadly—not because of a lost sale, but because of his unsatisfied curiosity. If anyone spoke to him, he would smile and reply. He would linger around, predict the next day's weather, open his bag and show his wares.

When he had walked the length of the Cape, Pierre would go back to his cabin, thinking about what he had seen, turning it over carefully in his mind. If he passed anyone on his way back, everyone in the village would be sure to hear that Pierre Le Rouge was talking to himself again, talking like a madman as he walked, and that loneliness must have addled his brains.

One morning Pierre killed a duck and caught several herring. It was the time of the March high tides: the young duck still had trouble taking off, and it had been easy. The gulf smelled of cod and salt. But fishing had been bad and his dam was almost empty. All the same, he decided to go to the Cape.

He wrapped everything in a cloth, then changed his mind. Someone had told him once that his game smelled of fish. He made up two packages and put them in his bag.

In the forest the pines were turning green; at the end of every bough three tiny fingers had sprouted. Slightly upturned, their needles a tenderer green than their neighbors of previous years, they filled the air with their sharp smell. It was always the same: the scent of the young pine shoots, and then it was summer. Soon they would grow darker in color, until they looked just like the other needles.

After the forest came the *savane*. Bunches of hemlock blossom stood shoulder high as Pierre walked across. He reached the low-lying mud flats, covered and exposed again each day by the tides. He knew just where the water would be at its lowest and he would be able to spare himself a lot of walking.

A crab tried to scuttle away. Pierre caught it, removed its legs, undid the package of herring, and put it inside. Farther on he dug up some clams that were squirting their waterballs in the sand. His bag was getting full, and time was passing. Finally he reached the Cape and began the uphill climb.

At the top is the gravel road. From there you can just see the summer people's houses through breaks in the trees. Pierre walked along the ditch to protect his old moccasins from the sharp-edged stones. Many of the houses were deserted, their windows and doors still boarded up, and Pierre went past. But some houses were open, people were sunbathing, a dog was barking.

Twice people called him over, and Pierre opened his bag for inspection. The second time, a woman took the duck, went to talk to someone in the gray house, came back with a dollar, and said, "Goodbye, Le Rouge. See you tomorrow perhaps? If you have another duck, I'll take that, too."

"I'll be back, I'll be back," said Pierre. "But then I won't be able to go back to the flat rock. Not for a month, at least, you understand."

The woman snorted. "What's he talking about? Mad as ever! Bye-bye, bye-bye!"

He left. He knew that if he killed another duckling for her, the mother duck would be wary of the flat rock, the one in front of the cabin, and she wouldn't bring her ducklings back in the morning anymore. He would have to go out to the end of the rocks and get one with his whip. He had seen his father hunt that way. Then he had tried, and it had worked. You had to stay completely still, then a good flick of the wrist, just as the lash was about to strike home—and the duck's head flew off, sliced clean.

Pierre went past all the other houses. Some looked dead at the end of their dark tunnels of foliage. From others, closer to the road, he heard music or voices. A woman waved to him. He reached the end of the Cape. Now the only house left was the white one, the one with the white fence whose gate was always off its hinges. I'll eat the herring myself, he thought, if nobody wants them. One of his feet hurt, and he stopped by the fence to see what was in his moccasin. Then he saw Marie. She was looking at him.

She was shaking with small sobs which she tried to disguise as she went on looking at Pierre. He wanted to smile, but he was too busy trying to see what was the matter. There was nobody about, and no danger either. She was wearing a straw-colored dress, her feet were small and bare on the grass, and as she wiped one cheek she made a face.

"Did you hurt yourself?" he asked.

She shrugged. He didn't understand.

"Why are you crying? I'm Le Rouge. . . . I have a few fish here. But . . . " He stopped because she had taken a small step backward.

"I've seen you," she said. "A lot. Last year, too. . . . So. You don't have to hurt yourself to cry. . . . You're bad," she went on. "And why do they call you 'Le Rouge,' anyway? Go away!"

"I don't know," said Pierre. He did not move. He looked at Marie and tried to think. "Animals cry, too," he said. "When they're hurt. . . . It's because of my hair."

"Are you making fun of me?" she said. "I don't believe you. So," she pouted. "And surely you have a name like everyone else?"

"My name is Pierre." Pierre. He realized that the only time he had pronounced the name out loud was when his parents were alive, never since. He couldn't get over the surprise of hearing his own name, and forgot to look at Marie. She was watching him closely.

"That's not very bright," she said. "They don't call me 'La Noire'!"

"It's because I'm Indian," he said.

"A red-haired Indian. That's a new one!"

"My mother was Indian. Half-Indian. Not my father."

He stopped. He wondered what it was he had forgotten to reply to. She had said something important, but what? He should have answered, and now he couldn't remember. Something was missing. It was unpleasant. Something was wrong. He looked at his foot, and wiggled it to ease the pain.

"So you have a mother, do you?" she said. "And a father?"

"Yes. Not anymore, they disappeared. People say they're dead. Everyone says so."

"Everyone says they're dead? What do you say?"

"No. Everyone has a mother and father."

"Well, I don't. So."

"And that's why you're crying."

"No, it isn't!" said Marie.

Pierre took off his moccasin and found what had been hurting him—a small twig rolling around under his sole. He took off both moccasins and put them in his bag. He could feel Marie's eyes following his movements.

He scratched his neck awkwardly and looked at the white house.

"So the people who live there aren't your parents?" he asked.

"No, they adopted me."

Had her parents disappeared as well? He thought of asking her, but didn't dare. And there was that thing she had said (which he couldn't remember); it still bothered him. Now Marie was looking at him very closely. It embarrassed him.

"You might as well leave now," she said. "It's no use going in. They won't buy anything from you. They're asleep. They've been drinking all night. So!"

She was still looking at him. Her eyes cut into him, shining, piercing, unwavering. He stepped back uncertainly.

"All right," he said. "I'll leave."

He turned and walked slowly away. He could feel her stare on his back. He went on. When he was a few steps from the open fence she called out suddenly: "But you can come back! My name is Marie!" she continued after a pause, and then: "See you again!"

He turned. She was still looking at him. He walked away.

Around four o'clock, when day begins, male raccoons start to make faint noises. They chatter and they dance nervous, rustling little steps, while chirping softly to their mates across the groves of birch and hazel. You notice it particularly at this time of the year, at the beginning of summer.

And now a female bustles over in answer to the summons. From his bed Pierre clearly hears her scuttle by. The chattering stops. She has reached her mate and is circling him so softly you can't hear a sound. It'll go on for a long time.

It is dawn outside. Crows and ravens converse endlessly, the echo of their harsh calls lingering in the unruly peaks of the tall black pines. The calls fade, two by two, then start up again a little farther on, a fainter echo repeating the rhythm. The salt smell of ferns drifts up to the cabin.

Had Pierre been sleeping? Dozing, more likely, since he had known, hour by hour, exactly how far the restless night had gone. He had heard all those sounds, sounds that usually went unnoticed— rustlings, creakings, calls. Just now he had distinctly heard every step in the battle between a fisher and a porcupine, although he hadn't understood what was happening until the moment of the kill.

With lightning speed the fisher had dropped out of his tree, head first as usual, and straight as an arrow, onto the porcupine. With one sweep of his claws he had turned the intruder over on his back. That's when you hear the faint scream and the snapping of jaws; that's how porcupines scream. This one didn't scream for long. The hungry fisher had quickly ripped open his soft, juicy belly.

It was at this moment that Pierre made up his mind. He would go and see Marie as soon as it was morning, as soon as he could, and try to talk to her again. But this time he would say more, and think about what he was saying. And this time he had to remember what to say to her and what he had to ask her. If he didn't, he'd look at Marie, then she'd speak, and he'd forget. He wondered why she had said, "You're bad." Was it because she was crying? Maybe she wasn't even thinking.

Why bad? he thought. She didn't mean it; she doesn't know. Who had she spoken to about him? Maybe the fishermen in the village; to her neighbors as well, the summer people on the Cape. That's who must have told Marie he was bad, because otherwise how could Marie know? She said she knew him, that she had seen him, last year, too. . . . It was very strange that he didn't remember her. . . . "Marie, Marie," he whispered. She'd been stony. With anger? She said they'd been drinking, and were asleep. They had adopted her. . . .

Pierre's bed was a mess. And the cover had lost its warmth; it had rolled inside out, the fur on the outside. He had tossed and turned too often. On any other night the high tide would have wakened him with the slap of waves against the rocks. But on this night the waters of the gulf only receded, and in silence.

He was sure a prowler had disturbed a sleeping skunk near the cabin around the middle of the night. He had heard nothing, but the strong smell of musk spray was everywhere. That's what must have happened. Around the middle of the night, the only time the seabirds are quiet. Even the petrels. The time when night stands still and freezes. But not for long. Then it tilts forward, and a new day begins. There is no light—except, sometimes, for the thin gleam of the aurora—but already yesterday is over. Then you hear only the wind, if there is any. Last night there wasn't. If you're awake, you hear the slightest sound, even the pad of the wolverine, lighter than a bird as he slinks along runs made by other animals, a robber of traps and spoiler of snares. A primitive creature, the wolverine, a glutton. The only hope you have of catching him is when he's stealing. Precisely at this time of night when anything can happen, when you can hear anything—even the pad of the wolverine.

In the depths of the night Pierre had listened. If he had heard the slightest rustling, if he had suspected a wolverine, perhaps he would have left the cabin to drive it away. But nothing stirred. The depths of the night were still. Only Marie inhabited this moment of silence. In her straw-colored dress. She also had on a white belt, Pierre thought. But he wasn't sure. What he was sure about, and could remember exactly, was Marie's legs and feet. They were slim, well-shaped legs without an ounce of fat on them, like the legs of a jumping animal, all slender muscle and bone within a tight, flawless envelope of skin. Her feet were small, in sandals whose open leatherwork revealed each one of the bones branching down to her toes, long toes with tender nails. Pierre turned over again, trying to recall her hands. What had Marie's hands looked like as she quickly brushed her cheek? He hadn't noticed. But her cheek, yes: it was very white, whiter even than her hand. And in the middle of that face, her eyes. Eyes like glittering metal, hard, piercing, staring unwaveringly at Pierre.

Even at nightfall Marie's eyes had been with him. At the time when cool air wafts the odor of seaweed into the cabin. And sleeping gulls wake on the water and squawk out their alarm, or their challenge to other males, before they settle down again with an occasional querulous cluck and drift back to sleep. And wingbeats, too: wood owls out hunting, and the ragged, crazy flight of petrels. It was around that time, when all nature grows drowsy, that Pierre had remembered. Marie had said, "You're bad." He should've asked her why, of course, but he hadn't.

What did being bad mean? It was important to

know, and Pierre studied the problem, his eyes wide open in the night, not seeing the planks of the cabin walls or the shelves where he stored his things. It was a serious matter. It was certainly serious for Marie. He frowned, trying to remember what his father used to say, that some animals were good. But no one had ever talked about bad ones when he was listening, if there were any. There were animals you weren't afraid of, the good ones probably. And there were the others, animals that bit, or clawed, or poisoned you— just like the plants his mother knew about. That kind was dangerous. But what about himself? How could he be dangerous?

He had stretched out on his bed at nightfall. Out on the rim of the gulf the setting sun had trailed long clouds of fiery ocher. Pierre had felt unusually tired, and sad in a way that was new to him. But as he began to doze a great peace stole through him. Gradually he felt better, calmer, more certain that he couldn't be dangerous. He would be able to smile at Marie. He would be able to look at Marie, listen to her, try to understand what she was saying. He thought that no one had ever made him want to speak and listen so much. He relaxed slowly, murmuring Marie's name with delight, and planning how he would see her again. Of course, the only way would be to go back to the white house and try again to sell fish or game to her parents. He would have to go to the beaver dam to see if his snares . . . He was falling asleep.

Earlier in the day, in the afternoon, he had spent all his time trying to echo Marie's words in his mind: "They don't call me 'La Noire'! That's not very smart. . . . " He had still been thinking of them as he watched the sun sink toward the gulf: "Everyone says they're dead? What do you say? Are you making fun of me?" He hadn't done any of the things he usually did in the afternoon. He hadn't fished, he had let the tide come in and flood his pen without even checking it. He hadn't gone to sell fish to the campers and find out what they were up to. He hadn't thought of these things. He hadn't even eaten. He had forgotten to go and catch that second duckling he promised the woman in the gray house. He had done nothing.

He had just sat on the stump in front of the cabin door, looking out at the sea. And he had thought about his meeting with Marie. It was almost low tide. Rocks streaked with rusty lichen smelled of dead leaves and sun. Smooth, round pebbles baked in the midday heat, scattered over the sand like eggs as far as the eye could see. Sticky strands of seaweed stretched over the beach, flat and interminable, like the skins of snakes long dead from exhaustion. Granite boulders lay where they had fallen along the shoreline, as smooth and livid as beached seals. Braids of tiny black mussel shells wound along the sand like terraces, marking each successive stage at which the outgoing tide had fingered. Pierre's fishpen was almost dry. In the open water beyond, a long-necked osprey was fishing. The smooth surface opened and closed with barely a ripple around each headlong drive. Long moments later the osprey bobbed up again, unruffled, some distance away.

All afternoon Pierre hadn't moved. Sitting there on the stump he had been drowning rapturously in the memory of Marie, his thoughts revolving slowly, vaguely, tenderly. He had been unable to move: it was a happiness he had never known before. Wherever he looked there was Marie. He reached back slowly through the yielding warmth as if he was bathing in the sun—a sun which seemed to grow bigger and warmer as time rolled farther and farther back. Back to the moment when Marie (perhaps she was smiling) had said: "But you can come back!" And she had given him her name, like a gift: "My name is Marie!" Then heard her last words, happier than all the rest. Yes, she had said it: "See you again." Again.

There hadn't been a breath of wind all afternoon. The gulf glittered all the way to the Iles. Marie's eyes. She had looked at him for a long time before she said that *See you again.* It was after she had said, "They're asleep. They've been drinking all night. So." Marie said, "So." She had said it several times, and the words brought back an old picture of his father, who also used it. His father also said, "So," but in a deeper voice.

The sun grew hotter and gulls appeared, as they did every day at low tide. They rose and fell lazily in the air at every movement of their wings. But Pierre could clearly see the glittering dot of each eye, sharp as a knifepoint, raking the beach and the shallows for a kill. His father used to throw them entrails and fish heads every day, yes, maybe every day, on this mud flat in front of the cabin. And even when there was nothing to eat the gulls still flew in and settled on the rocks and in the trees. Since Pierre had been on his own, they came only occasionally. They had forgotten, or else they were different gulls.

Today he could have tossed them the dead herring when he got back to the cabin. But he hadn't done anything. He was thinking of what Marie had said: "You're bad." She had also said, "Go away!"—something Pierre had never heard before. That was it. That was what Pierre had forgotten, that's what he should have replied to when he was with Marie. He had remembered it on his way back from the white house, in the middle of the forest, just before he reached the pines. He had walked on without seeing anything.

Too late. It had been too late to answer and to ask Marie what she had meant. He had already been far from the Cape, cutting across the mud flats on his way back to the cabin. He had felt alone, and crushed.

3

He had never gone to the Cape two days in a row. The track was torturous and rough. Of course, there was the well-trodden forest path, starting at the cabin and clearly marked among the ferns and pine. And at the other end, after you crossed the mud flats, you reached the road leading up to the Cape. But in between these two short stretches was natural chaos. The track changed constantly. Winds had littered the rocky floor with fallen trees; rainstorms had flooded a stretch of *savane,* suddenly transforming it into bog and swampy marshland.

Nevertheless, he set out for the Cape as soon as it was morning, without losing any time. He emptied his birch-bark bag and left the herring behind, taking only some clams wrapped in paper. He walked quickly.

The shadows were just turning pale under the trees, whose tops were bathed in bright sunlight. At the forest edge, the light exploded over prairie flowers. The gulf was a carpet of sparkling wavelets all the way to the horizon where an early-morning haze veiled the Iles-aux-Ours.

Pierre trod on, mindless of the rough track, mindless of the beauty around him, mindless of everything but Marie. Perhaps she was by the white fence. Perhaps she was talking to neighbors. He'd show them his clams. But he wouldn't speak to her because of the people there.

Perhaps she'd be alone. Yes, he would speak to her. "You said I could come back," he said aloud. He looked up at the sky. "Yes, that's what I'll say."

Pierre walked on, the smile on his face slowly changing to a creased frown. What if she wasn't there? He'd go through the fence to the white house. He'd knock, but it would be the man who had adopted her. He'd recognize him, small, dark-haired, with a beard. He'd say, "I have clams here, if you want. One dollar." And then maybe he'd see Marie. He wondered if she would be crying.

He walked along the high-water mark, skirting every inlet. He walked as fast as he could, reached the Cape road and walked on under the high trees. A smell of resin wafted from last year's stumps.

Someone was watching him from the doorstep of the gray house with green shutters. A young man Pierre had never seen before; he had no time to look at him now. A car overtook him, covering the road and the undergrowth with dust; a little later another went by. He went on, his pace unchanging, toward the

25

white house at the tip of the Cape. And toward Marie, who was there. She waved. She was wearing tan pants and a sweater. As he got closer he saw that she was carrying a book and that her feet were bare in the grass by the side of the road.

Pierre smiled.

"You're not crying today," he said.

"I wasn't crying yesterday. Well, not really crying. It was . . . it was nothing."

"I thought about you. I hoped you would be here. You said I could come back." He looked at his feet, then added awkwardly, "And there's something I wanted to ask you."

"Come a little closer. You can come in, you know. They're not here. And what if they were? They've gone to get something to eat or drink or whatever. If we sit behind those rocks there, no one will see us. I like it here. Come and look. I go there to read so no one will bother me. If they come back, you can get away down there, by the water. Come on."

"But I brought some shellfish. I could sell them some. I had them yesterday, but no one wanted any."

"No. You're not to sell them anything. Anything, you understand?" she said with unusual force, then seeing the stunned look on his face, she explained: "If they see you with me, I'm the one who'll get it. 'What were you doing, you have no business with Le Rouge, why don't you behave properly?' They go on and on at me, they fight. She takes my side and he shouts. Or the other way round, but it's just the same. They shout, and break things, and she cries. I shut myself up with a book or I go for a walk in the woods and pick flowers and strawberries. I like being down by the sea. I watch the gray seagulls land in the water. I could spend hours there. . . . But I prefer it when they haven't been fighting. Because then, when I go back, they're drunk and they jump on me. So!"

"So!" said Pierre, and smiled.

He followed Marie around the house. She led the way under the trees and squeezed between two giant granite rocks. There a landslide had left a sort of flat clearing, encased on three sides by heaped boulders. On the open side was a wooded slope leading down to the gulf. You could see the water through the low-hanging hemlock boughs.

"Isn't it nice?" said Marie. "No one can see us."

"You know, if they light in the water and they're gray, they're not seagulls, they're herring gulls."

"Is that so? I didn't know, Come, sit down."

"Why did you say I'm bad?"

"Did I say that? You are bad, aren't you?"

"What does it mean, bad?"

"Oh, come on. You don't understand bad? I don't believe you."

"No, I know what you mean. But why . . . "

"It's because you kill animals. That's one way of being bad. For you. All you do is kill. That's what people say. Animals, birds, fish. I don't think the fish worry me so much. Do fish feel it when you kill them? I think they must, but I don't think I feel so bad about it. But the other animals, that's horrible!

"Take seals," she went on. "Even the little white pups. You skin them! Uggh! And marten, and mink, and beaver, and all the animals in the woods and the

27

gulf. You go over to the Iles, you go over to the far shore, you go everywhere. You're cruel to them. So!"

"So!"

"Everyone knows. They told me. I asked them what you did all through the year, all your life, and they told me. But they don't know how to tell anything straight. They get all mixed up and act dumb. They seem to think there's nothing wrong with it. They're stupid and ignorant."

She paused briefly, bit her lower lip and turned to Pierre. "He said, 'Le Rouge has to live, doesn't he?' That just made me mad." She went on. "'Look at her, she's crying, the little idiot! Real little tenderheart, only she hasn't got a heart. The kid's a bundle of nerves! She shouldn't be worrying about such things at her age. At thirteen I knew all there was to know about life, but that didn't stop me thinking about art. . . . About *something*, for heaven's sake! But look at her! A complete blank! She looks at one of my paintings and she sees nothing! She's a failure, a hundred-percent failure. All she does is read . . . she reads everything, anything, and naturally she understands nothing! To think I adopted that! What a joke!'" Marie grimaced, then continued in a monotone, "'Just shut that filth up! She's mine, and anyway, you were perfectly willing to take her on. And when have you ever done anything to help her?' 'Well, what about you? Let's talk about you! The only time you think of her is when there's no one else around—about once in a blue moon!' 'That's just not true. Anyway, instead of helping her, you try and destroy her.' 'I have better things to do than waste my

28.

time discussing childish garbage. *I* work!' 'Hah! How many years is it since you produced anything, eh? Don't make me laugh! Work! That's a pretty fancy name for those miserable little brushstrokes you manage once in a while. And your pals—whee! Now that's what I really call work!' 'You weren't so critical of my miserable little brushstrokes a few years ago, were you? And at least I sell? Oh, let's have a drink. You make me laugh!' 'People will buy anything these days.'

"Finally he kicks a chair or a table to pieces. They yell and laugh like crazy people. Other times she's the one who's nasty about me. She's even dumber than he is. When she's had a lot to drink, or when she's been away for a few days, she tells me I'm ugly and dishonest and I love nobody. That sort of thing. . . . So!"

"So!"

"Why do you kill animals, Pierre?"

"Wait . . . I've never thought about it."

"You should think. You should read. Then you'll learn, you'll learn everything. Everything's in books. What a pity, because you interest me, Pierre. When you smile, specially when you smile. You look nice, you're like a nice thin dog. I'd like to have a dog, you know? Or a cat. But they won't let me. Do you have a dog?"

"No."

"You should. He'd keep you company. Then you'd love him. And maybe you'd get to love other animals, too. Little by little. So!"

"So. You always say 'so.' "

"What do you mean, so? Are you making fun of me?"

"No, no," said Pierre. "I'm thinking of my father. He used to say 'so' the same way. My father had a dog."

"That's good. Well, he didn't kill it, did he?"

"No. The dog pulled the sled. That's how I know they went through the ice. I've often thought about it. The dog didn't come back. That means he died for sure."

"What ice? What are you talking about?"

"When my parents went away, with the dog, and were lost. . . . My father taught me how to kill animals. He showed me all the ways. You put skunk in a sack and drown them. You hold a fox round the neck with one hand and squeeze his hind legs between your thighs. Then you press his heart downward with the other hand, and he dies," Pierre said, making the act more explicit with his hand gestures.

"That's disgusting!"

"You kill otter by hitting them on the nose with a log," Pierre went on, again gesturing with his hands. "For lynx you need a snare. They strangle themselves: that way the pelt isn't damaged. And my father taught me how to use a whip and lay snares. I have a jackrabbit run. I put young birch boughs down the middle, good tender ones. Jackrabbit love them. They come inside, and when they leave, they snare themselves."

"That's what being bad is."

"I didn't know." Pierre was crestfallen.

"My poor Pierre, you can be bad without knowing it. . . . Shh!! A car coming up the road! Maybe it's them. You can leave that way. . . . No, it stopped."

Marie sighed with relief. "It's the neighbors. Stay a bit longer."

"I hear children running," Pierre said.

"You do? You can hear them? Wow! Well, it must be the neighbors, then. You know, Pierre, I think you're not bad, and I didn't mean to hurt your feelings."

"But you can be bad without knowing it. You said so."

"Uh-huh, not you. I can tell. People say you can predict the weather as well. What's it going to be like tomorrow?"

"Tomorrow? Wind, a lot of wind after the evening tide. There'll be waves, the water will be muddy, maybe there'll be plaice in my dam."

"But how can you tell?" Marie's eyes were wide with astonishment.

"Oh, things. The sea, the aspen leaves. . . . The gulls, the way they fly. . . . Habit. . . . I don't know, really. But I'm often wrong."

"They say you're never wrong. But they also say all sorts of things about you. They say you eat raw meat. And live shrimp! They say you're mad and you do crazy things. I don't think so. You haven't said one dumb thing, not one."

"I don't know. I like talking, but it's hard," said Pierre. "Often I talk to myself. Or I talk to the trees and the sea. It's hard."

"Very. But you're right. They can't say dumb things back. Do you meet many people?"

"Hardly anybody. Except the Voyageur. He comes by a lot."

"You know what I think? I think they're afraid of you! They say you live in a terrible place, so far away, they say you could kill somebody, they say all kinds of things, but I think they're a little scared of you. So! . . . Do you sell them furs?" she asked.

"Yes. Mostly to the Voyageur. I trade with him as well. He has everything in his truck."

"Even in winter?"

"Yes. When the snow's too deep, he stops a little way off, over behind the maples. I hear him and I see his lights. I put on my snowshoes and go out to meet him. But he doesn't come often in winter. And I sometimes see hunters and fishermen, and people from the village who come by once in a while. And campers, over by the shore near my place. . . ." He smiled. "Raw meat . . . it's good," Pierre went on. "Not all the meat, of course, but . . ."

"It doesn't matter. Forget it. I like being here with you."

She looked as though a wave had washed gently over her. Or as though her whole body were slowly filling with the long, deep breath she drew as she closed her eyes. The lids were a soft, creamy white. Then she opened her eyes again and stared ahead without moving. She let herself slip into the softness of the surrounding grass. Pierre was squatting beside her in his customary position, legs tucked beneath him. His bag, slung from his shoulder by a leather strap, hung to the ground. Marie looked at this man in his checked woolen jacket and ancient pants. His hair was red, his face, weatherbeaten, and his eyes were a very pale blue—two skies that could cloud over

32

without warning. His lips were curved in the faintest of smiles.

They could hear seabirds calling nearby, probably from the shore a little below their hideaway in the rocks. Through the tree trunks the gulf stretched to the horizon, where the Iles looked as if they were sailing slowly through the haze.

After a moment Pierre said, "I don't understand everything you say. But if you speak some more, I'm sure I'll understand. If you explain."

"Of course I will. Things just need explaining, and I'm good at that. Once he said I was a genius. Oh, I know it was to make fun of me, but that doesn't matter. He was mad, too. 'She's impossible,' he said. 'She knows everything, she's read everything, she's old, old as the hills! You're an old woman! She argues, she explains, she drives us crazy, oh, man!'" She looked up at Pierre. "But what didn't you understand?" she asked.

"I don't know. Him. I don't understand him."

"Him? When I was small, I was scared of him. I listened to him. I heard him shout, and I was scared. And I thought the things he said were right. I was like you, I didn't understand everything. . . . They quarreled about things I didn't understand. I was too young. They fought, too. I heard them hitting each other and breaking things. I hate noise, you know. Even when they laughed out loud, I could still hear the noises and I was scared." She paused and took a deep breath. Her hands were stretched out on the grass; clumps of green blades sprouted through her fingers. She looked at Pierre and said, "Reading was the only thing I liked. I found quiet spots like this one, see, and I just read. The more things I read, the more things I understood—the books explained them. And you know what? I found that he wasn't right. 'That's not true,' I told him. Pow! He was mad. So was she. 'Don't argue,' she used to say. But the more I found out, the more I read, and the more I found out all over again. In the end I knew everything (so he said!). I didn't really know everything, you know, but enough to answer him back. Since then he's hated me. And I hate him. You understand?"

"I think so. A little. . . . For you, it's like being in a trap," said Pierre. "Only you've found out how to slip through without getting caught."

"Say, that's not stupid! That's right!"

"If a wolverine finds a trap, he gets away with the bait. He's a real cunning one."

"Yes? Well, that's the same thing."

"But why the trap?" asked Pierre.

"I don't know, but I'll know some day, and then I'll know everything. . . . Look at you, your father taught you how to kill animals. Couldn't he have taught you something else? I don't know what. But I know that he wasn't right, either. How can you kill animals! They can't fight back. It's not fair."

"But they'd die anyway."

"That's a good one! You're going to die too! But do I kill you?"

"I don't hurt them. I hide and wait. They don't see me, they aren't even scared, they don't suspect anything. Just one shot and it's over. It's even quicker with the whip."

34

"Yes, and you set traps and lay snares, don't you? And the animal gets caught and strangles itself...."

"It's over very quick."

"Or else it gets caught in a trap, and suffers until you come and kill it. It's disgusting!"

"Animals kill each other. They really hurt each other, you know."

"Huh!"

"They do! They eat each other alive. Like me with shrimp."

"Ugghh!"

"Yes, straight into the guts with their teeth! Sometimes moose drag their intestines along for days before they die."

"Shut up, Pierre, you're making me sick."

Marie's hands were on her knees. Her fingers made tiny bridges that arched away from their own bluish shadows. Around one of them was a thin silver ring on which a small orange stone glowed softly. Pierre could see the shape of the bones radiating down the backs of her hands. Branching blue veins followed the rise and fall of each miniature ravine under a fine, sun-bleached down. Below, held tightly together, her ankles protruded from the pants, and the interplay of small bones began again under her skin, all the way to the toes, which were pressed down into the sand and grass.

Marie had put her book beside her. She was leafing through it and looking at Pierre. After a while she said, "Listen, I'll lend you my book. That'll be better than talking like this. It's very interesting. I haven't finished it, but you can give it back whenever you

35

want. I have lots of others in the meantime. Every time I go to the store with her I bring a whole pile back. She doesn't care. She says, 'At least you won't be bothering me!' That's what *she* says!"

She smiled at Pierre; her eyes were twinkling with enthusiasm. "You know what it's about?" she said. "It's a fantastic story. It's about this very wicked man who kills his mother and father, just to get his inheritance sooner, you understand. And he's horribly cruel to everyone. He has this vicious smile, really evil, and his eyes blaze with fury! He's very rich, he buys bunches of slaves, he beats them, even though they're tired and sick. And listen to this"—Marie read from the book—"'Even their teeth, the splendid white teeth of those once-happy Negroes, fell out one by one.' It's fabulous, I tell you! And he really is the most wicked man. He's horrible to anyone who stands in his way. . . . Anyway, at the end, when they've had enough of him, this man, when they know about all the horrible things he's done, he falls deathly ill. And no one will look after him, see, they're too afraid of him! His punishment is dreadful. He suffers horribly, and dies with the name of Satan on his lips. I'm telling you! It's a good book, believe me."

Marie turned to the end of the book, to the last page, facing the cover, and showed him the final words. "I know the whole story," she said, "because I've read the end. I couldn't help it. . . . But all those adventures before he dies. It's tremendous, it's fantastic. . . . It's silly, I know, I've read the ending. But I keep wondering what's going to happen next! Don't you believe me?"

"Yes. I think I understand that."

36

"Do you want it?"

"The book?"

"Of course. I'll lend it to you, I tell you I have others. Just give it back, that's all. You'll see, it's very good. Put it in your bag . . . wait, I'll help you. Ugghh! How disgusting! You're still carrying those ghastly things?"

"They're clams," said Pierre.

"You can come and see me tomorrow, but don't bring anything. So!"

"Okay," said Pierre, and smiled.

Marie looked at him, and suddenly she smiled, too. She plucked a blade of grass and put it in her mouth.

She glanced toward the white house. They could barely see one corner which was made of overlapping white planks and supported on a stout wooden pillar. The upper part of the corner was hidden by the leaves of a birch, and the bottom by the rocks they had squeezed through to enter the clearing.

"What you *can* bring tomorrow," said Marie, "is flowers. Or any plants you know. They say you know which ones are good to eat and which are poisonous. Is that right?"

"I know a lot of them. My mother Nod showed me. I'll bring some. Good ones or poisonous?"

"I'd prefer poisonous ones, just to see. . . . Listen, a car! This time it *is* them! Go down that way. See you tomorrow, if you can come. I'll be waiting here. Hurry!"

She had jumped up and was already running away. Motionless, Pierre listened as a car drove up in front of the house.

As soon as Marie was out of sight he got up, shouldered his bag, and went off as quietly as he could down the slope and toward the sea. His bare feet made a faint rustling as he walked. Down by the water, in the lee of the Cape, he took his moccasins from his pockets and put them on to walk along the pebbled shore.

Farther on, when he was certain that no one could see or hear him from the white house, he cut into the high forest and climbed back to the road.

He walked homeward slowly.

He did not want to see anyone.

He walked at an even pace, head slightly lowered as usual. He was full of Marie, of this day, of the words they had exchanged. His thoughts were crowded.

He thought about marten, jackrabbit, seals. And about birds.

He thought about the beaver traps he had set, near the dam behind his cabin.

He thought about his father and about raw shrimp, which tasted so good.

As he crossed the swampland he looked around absentmindedly for the black grass his mother Nod hated so much, the kind that made you vomit. He wanted to get some for Marie, but he didn't see any. It was not the right season. It would only just be coming up under the wormwood and hemlock. A flowering bunch of the grass that smelled of sloes.

He sat down on the stump in front of his door. He began to think of Marie. Tomorrow, she had said. The same place. "I'll be waiting here." That's what she had said.

A little later he rose and went inside. He picked up his bag and turned it out on the table.

He opened the clams with a knife and ate them one by one. He drank a cup of water. There was the book beside him. Pierre looked at it. He sat down in front of it, and began to turn the pages, one after another, slowly. When he had finished, he closed the book.

Next day, he went back to the white house, slipped between the rocks and entered the clearing. There was Marie. She was playing with pebbles laid out in rows. She was moving them around very quickly, as if following an elaborate calculation or a mysterious pattern that she alone knew. She put several stones together, then separated them, then regrouped them in a different way, then removed one or two from the group. Her hands never stopped moving. She looked up and said, "It's you. Hello. You came."

"Here's the book," said Pierre.

"Already? Have you read it? Have you begun it?"

"No."

"Why?"

"I can't read," said Pierre. He smiled.

"Even mutes learn to read," said Marie. "It's easy. They just make signs with their fingers for each letter of the alphabet. So it can't be that hard for someone who can talk. He can go much faster if he just listens to what he's told, and memorizes the shape of each letter."

"I don't say it's hard. I just don't know. I'm a bit scared."

"So! You're scared without even knowing."

"Once you know, you're not scared anymore."

"Do you think so? That's funny, what you just said. It's when I know that I start to get scared. Like when I go to the dentist. I can't stand dentists, they scare me, and I don't want to know which day I have to go. If I do, I have nightmares."

"I've never been to a dentist."

"No? Wow!"

Marie wrinkled her nose as she peered at Pierre's lips. She didn't believe him. She made him open his mouth—"Just to see. . . . Come on, open!" But Pierre was roaring with laughter and she couldn't see them properly. After several such attempts, Pierre finally revealed magnificent, flawless teeth. Marie was astounded.

"Anyway," she went on, "when I go down to the village with her I'll bring you a book. I'll hide it in among mine. A spelling book or a primer, that's how people learn to read. (She won't care; she never notices.) She lets me buy all the books I want while she's getting her true-love magazines. . . .

"Oh, of course, you don't know what those are!" she said, seeing the puzzled look on his face. "My poor Pierre, you don't know a thing. . . . She eats them up, but at least that means she leaves me in peace. She says, 'At least you won't be bothering me'—but it's really *her* that's not bothering *me!* Sometimes she stays away for two days and nights: those are the times I like best. Then, when I get hungry, I drink milk and eat eggs. Do you like raw eggs? You make two holes with a needle, you suck, and you swallow. It's good. Or I eat whatever I find in the icebox. He says she leaves to take her movie cure (that's because she was once in the movies). You should see the scenes when she comes back! That's the only bad part—when she comes back. I'm happy when she gets dressed to go away because then I know I'm going to be happy for a long time. But I also know that later . . . more yelling and screaming. . . ."

"Raw eggs are like shrimp. They're good."

"When we're here at the Cape, it's even better, because then they both leave together to whoop it up with the neighbors. The people next door."

"With the two children?"

"The two idiots, yes."

She wrinkled her face in disgust. Pierre stared at her wide-eyed, trying to understand what she meant. At the same time he couldn't help noticing that Marie's face smelled of sugared apples.

"Oh, forget it!" she said. "You know you don't understand everything."

"But you said you'd explain..."

"Explain what? They're dumb. So! Real babies! They call me 'orphan.' They jeer and throw stones at me. One day last year they jumped on me and tried to pull my dress off. I was small last year, you understand? I ran away and found a long stick. Then I hid and jumped out on them. Wow, did I give it to them!"

"Are children bad?"

"Of course. And they yell like lunatics all the time. Another day," Marie rambled on, "they had a party; it went on all night. Next morning the two idiots were screaming. I went to look. They were outside, crying like babies. You know why? They couldn't find anything to eat in the kitchen, and they were scared, the stupid little idiots. I went into the house and looked in all the rooms upstairs. It was a mess. There were bottles and glasses and plates everywhere. Everyone was asleep upstairs. Downstairs, too.... I didn't even know some of the people they'd invited. They were ugly, and I left. I left the two idiots to look after themselves. They're dumb! So!"

42

"Does learning to read take long?"

"No. I don't know, I can't remember. I was young, you understand? I bet you can't even count, if such a thing is possible."

"I can, a little."

"Oh, yes? I bet you can't add then. What's two and two?" she asked.

Pierre looked at her blankly.

"So!" said Marie. "It's just incredible...

"So you never went to school?" she persisted.

"Are you going to answer or not? Wasn't there a school in the village?"

"No, it was in the next village," said Pierre. "They came to get the children in a wagon. I think it was a wagon. Now there's a school, and buses."

"I know that. But why didn't you go?" she said.

"I can't remember. I was very young. I can't remember. But I do remember there was no road, because my father had to go a long way on his snowshoes in winter to get supplies or sell pelts. Sometimes he took my mother. Later on, when the campers started to come to the beach, there at the end of the bay, they put in a road, but only for the summer. But I was already big. Quite big. That's when the Voyageur started to call in his truck. And other people came to see my father—fishermen and hunters. Not very often."

"They should have," said Marie.

"Should have what?"

"Sent you to school. I'm not at all pleased with your father, you know. What did he say about school? And about learning to read?"

"I can't remember."

"They're all the same. They read the newspaper, and that's it."

"Do you think I could read the newspaper, too?"

"Papers are stupid, there's nothing in them. You'll find out. But when you read books, then . . . !"

"My father didn't read the paper," said Pierre.

"Of course not, buried out there in the woods."

"But he had an envelope with pieces of newspaper in it. He used to take them out and read them. Just a little, not for long. Then he would put them back without saying anything. I remember that. And I still have the envelope," Pierre added after a pause.

"But no books, of course?"

"So, if I could read, I'd open the envelope and I'd know what he was reading. Afterward, he said nothing, he just thought. I remember that very well. And then he went out into the woods alone, for a long time, and my mother and I just sat and waited for him."

"Bring me the envelope and I'll read it to you. You mean you never said to him, 'I want to learn to read'? And he never mentioned it?"

Pierre looked at Marie. The other children he'd seen weren't like Marie. They blubbered, they stared at everything, they made faces, they never stopped moving. They picked up stones and threw them at him, then they ran away. They hit each other with sticks, they broke branches, they lost their tempers. But Marie was sitting there looking at him. Why was she crying? he wondered. "You don't have to hurt yourself to cry." That's what she had said the other day. . . .

44

Marie always listened to Pierre, although she sometimes looked as if she didn't. She seemed to reach out, almost furtively, for certain words that interested her, the way you look round quickly when a sudden noise attracts you or intrigues you. She snatched at the words. She added them to her own thoughts, which drew new life from them and which never seemed to flag. At other times she watched Pierre secretly, noting the smallest details of his clothes, his face, his hands. At these times he would feel a little disturbed and would break off in the middle of what he was saying. She would notice it at once and look away, pretending to be absorbed in a plant, a tree, the gulf, or a passing bird. And Pierre knew she did this on purpose to make him feel better. Yes. Pierre knew. And it did feel better. He felt like going on, like talking more, like listening. Especially listening, listening to Marie.

When she talked about her parents and what they said, she adopted a small, childlike tone without highs or lows, and talked very fast, as if she were reciting unconnected, meaningless words. A noise. Like the tiny bubbling of a spring. Pierre found it funny; it made him laugh every time. But when she was explaining something, her voice became insistent, with a modulated rhythm that slightly exaggerated the effect of her words—as if she wanted it clearly understood where the importance lay for her, and how unchallengeable that importance was. Uncertainty, it was clear, would have irritated her. She reminded him of a tiny red and white chipmunk, no bigger than two walnuts as it stands erect—well out of harm's way on a high branch—and chatters out a flood of insults to impress on an intruder that its size should in no way be confused with its courage. A chipmunk's voice is a formidable weapon. It can drive a lynx away.

"You look angry, my poor Pierre," she said. "I can tell you don't want to answer."

"You know everything, you do," said Pierre.

"No, I don't! What an idea! I told you, it's because I can read. First I learn, then I explain to you, and that makes you mad."

"I learn," said Pierre, "and then I forget. When I listen to the radio, I think I've learned something, but I forget it right away. Then I wonder if I really understood, and things get difficult, and then I don't know anymore."

"That's because you started out all wrong. It's the way you were raised, I tell you. You have a lot of catching up to do. It's unbelievable."

Pierre said nothing.

"I didn't start out right, either," she went on, "but that didn't stop me doing what I wanted to do. In kindergarten they said they couldn't do anything with me. 'You're too proud, Marie. Come off your high horse.' 'Call me *vous*, not *tu*,' I said. 'Well, listen to her! Who does she think she is?' And who did they think they were? They were liars, they made up all kinds of incredible lies all the time. Argumentative, they said I was—but *they* never stopped arguing! Idiots, I'm telling you. . . . But they leave me alone now that I'm in high school. There are too many of us, and no one bothers you. So I can read."

"You're better than the radio."

"I should think so!"

"I don't listen to it much since I met you. Not

46

yesterday or the day before. Since I spoke to you. I thought of you all the time."

"Me, too," said Marie. "In the evening and at night as well. I lay in bed and I didn't even read. I couldn't wait until morning. You know why? To see you."

For several minutes now they had heard the lazy throb of an engine. It seemed to come from the water. Marie cocked her head. "Do you hear?" She got up and peered through the trees.

"It's the towboat," said Pierre. "It's coming down on the tide." He got up, too, and stood with Marie at the edge of the slope overlooking the river.

Heavy-bellied under its two stubby masts, the ship slid into view. Its decks were overloaded with piles of logs that rose higher than the bridge. The air was so clear that even at this distance they could see the outline of the helmsman in his glassed-in cabin. The ship's wake was a dark, gently heaving line against the glass-smooth surface. Gulls hung watchfully over it, seemingly motionless. The reclining shapes of the Iles swam together in one long, dark mass on the horizon. Here and there a lighter patch marked a beach or a clearing. Marie looked toward the Iles.

"I would like to go there," she said. "We could."

"If we had a boat," said Pierre. "Or in winter, but not very often, you know."

"Oh."

She was lost in her own thoughts. "Talk to me," she said suddenly.

"What about?"

"Anything. I like to hear you talk. About animals . . ." She was gazing toward the gulf without really seeing anything. She didn't move. Pierre looked

47

at her, at the smooth line of her cheek, at the wisps of hair caressing her face. It's like that day when I saw her by the fence, crying, he thought. She was pushing out her mouth that same way, her lips a thin line that curved upward to the left and ended in a tiny dimple. She was frowning a little, and blinking in the sun.

"This morning I found a weasel's hide," said Pierre, breaking away from his thoughts. "In an old jack-rabbit burrow. Then I went down to the stream for water and found some turtle eggs."

"Did you eat them?"

"Yes."

"Is that all?" Marie said. "You don't tell stories well."

"Will you be here tomorrow?"

"Of course."

He wanted to tell her something else. But what? He looked at her. But she had turned round. She still seemed to be dreaming. Then she woke up suddenly and in a few steps she was on the other side of the clearing. She stopped behind a rock, turned toward Pierre, waved, and ran. She was gone before he had time to think.

She had been thinking about it for three days. When he had told her, she hadn't been able to believe it. She'd been amazed. *He can't read!* Wow! Incredible! She had not known what to say. And as for Pierre, he had known that she hadn't dared to ask him any more questions. And he hadn't said anything else, either. He had been stunned by this revelation which had come to him the moment he had admitted it. And when he had seen Marie's amazement, its full impact had hit him: *He couldn't read.*

She should have guessed. Living out there in the wilds. She had taken his secret with her, a secret that kept her silent all day, a secret whose pages she slowly turned that night. Until she fell asleep.

All next day her thoughts had wandered abruptly. A gesture broken off midway. A dash across the grass suddenly abandoned for no reason, forgotten as she absently plucked a blade of grass. When she saw Pierre again, when he showed up faithfully at the house, his coming by now habitual, and sat down at the same spot behind the rocks, she had looked at him without saying a word. They hardly spoke.

"I don't know what's wrong," she said. "I'm looking at you. And trying to think." He asked her, "Tell me more, I like listening to you." She answered, "Yes, yes, wait... I don't really want to, you know. I'm thinking." She didn't stay long, she soon left. But first she said, "Tomorrow you'll see. Come at the same time and I'll have a surprise for you."

"The first thing I learned was vowels," said Marie. "So you can start the same way. If you know the vowels, and there aren't many, all you have to do is string them together with the other letters and you'll be able to make all the words you want. Now, I've got this book for you. It's a spelling book. Everything I have to tell you is on each page. So you see I can't go wrong. It's really simple: all I have to do is read it and then teach you. See how useful it is?"

Pierre looked at the book in her hands. This one had big letters and drawings and colors.

"Right then, vowels," she continued. "Sit up straight and concentrate. Look, the first one is A. Take a good look. See? A."

"Oh... is that it?"

"Of course. Easy, isn't it? So far! It comes to a point at the top, with a crossbar, like... like... like an arrow! That's the capital A, the big A. Let's just call it big, so you'll understand. I'll explain later about capitals and where you have to put them. But for now we'll just remember the names of the letters. This is the small *a*, the real one. A little circle with a tail like a cat. . . . I wish I had a cat."

Pierre began to laugh. He looked at Marie, but she was suddenly serious, almost haughty. She had entered a world of whose importance she had no doubt. "Say it," she told him. Pierre said it.

"Here's another *a*. This one is for books and newspapers. You and I never have to write it: it's just for reading. It's still a cat with a tail, but prettier, see? With a head, and a body too. And they've drawn a cat beside it. That's smart. But since you don't know anything, we're not going to learn the word 'cat,' because if we do, we'll be here all day."

"Okay," said Pierre.

"Sure you understand?"

"Yes. What comes next?"

"You're going too fast. You'll never remember. Okay, next page. This one is *E*. Like a fork, see? It's the capital *E*, the big one, like the big pointed *A*. This one here is the real *e*. It's a loop, the kind you make with a rope, I suppose, when you're making a knot. Now, repeat after me: *e, e* . . ."

Pierre watched her lips and repeated the sound.

"And here's the same letter for reading. The rope's too short, a piece is missing, but it's the same loop."

Pierre looked at the *e* with the missing piece and frowned.

"You said you wanted to learn," she said sternly. "You *said* so! So I'm teaching you. I told you it was terribly difficult. And anyway, you *have* to learn. How can you go through life not being able to read?"

Pierre looked up and said: "I understand. There are two kinds of letters, letters you read and letters you write."

"And capitals, the big ones," said Marie. "For beginning a sentence, for beginning proper names. . . . Uhh. But that's not important."

"And the ones for reading are in newspapers?"

"Of course."

"I want to learn the newspaper ones. Go on."

Marie turned the pages. She said: "This is *i*. It's the funniest one, it has a dot on top. A hat. No, it's a man with a head. Go on, say it."

"Is this one for reading, too?"

"Yes, look, it's even easier."

"Okay, what comes next?"

"No, you have to say it! That's not the way to learn! If you don't work at it, it doesn't do any good." Marie was getting annoyed. Pierre said: "*i, i, i*..." Marie watched him closely. She said, "I bet you've forgotten already. Let's see." She turned back the pages and showed him the letters, and Pierre read "*a*," then "*e*." Marie said nothing.

While she seemed to be dreaming, or perhaps thinking about the worth of her method, Pierre reached out and began to leaf through the book, slowly reading each letter in a low voice. Then he said, "This is how you learn to read?"

"Of course."

"Good. Let's go on."

"Wait. I want to make sure we're doing it properly."

"Okay."

"Yes, okay. You keep saying 'okay': You act as if

you'll do anything I say, but I wonder how much you'll remember.... Anyway, let's go on. This is *o*. Round. Like your lips when you say it. That's what they told me when I was young, and I liked it. *O*, like the sun. Try it."

"Look, look! The reading one is round as well!"

"I know that!" said Marie. "I can read, you know!"

That afternoon she showed Pierre all the vowels, her outstretched finger tracing the outline of each letter in the spelling book as she explained its shape to him.

They were so engrossed that they did not notice the slow passage of the sun as it dipped toward the clouds on the rim of the gulf, or the flocks of duck skimming low across the water, or the busy sounds coming from the summer people on the Cape.

Marie tried everything: she picked pages at random, jumped back and forth in the book, hid letters with her hand—print, then calligraphy, then capitals. But Pierre came up with the right sound for every letter every time. She finally closed the book and declared that they had done enough for the day. Pierre noticed that a breeze had sprung up and that the tide was coming in. He was surprised.

"Soon you should start writing," said Marie. "But what a job it'll be if I start you with a pencil and paper now. I bet your fingers are clumsy. Which is best—learning to read all the letters first, or writing a few as well, just to try them out? In school, I remember . . . And then there's groups of letters. You should really do both to understand properly. . . . I know! Wait a second."

She jumped up and ran to the white house. She was

back a moment later with a page from a newspaper which she gave to Pierre. She was out of breath.

"Look for all the letters you know there," she said. "There are lots of them. Then you can show them to me. You have to be sure you recognize them, otherwise it won't do any good. Because tomorrow it'll be a lot harder."

Pierre carried the paper home with great care. He often picked up newspapers or magazines at the campsite or in the bins the summer people left by the road in front of their houses every week. He used them for all kinds of things: wrapping up fish and game; making fires; keeping the seeds from his vegetable garden till spring. He used to study their pages curiously, particularly the photographs. He liked the color photos a lot. Almost all of them were a mystery to him, and the hours he spent poring over them gave him pleasure for days. Only when he had finally reached a conclusion as to their meaning and subject did he use the newspaper and burn it.

But this one! He hardly dared close his fingers over it; he carried it with infinite care.

As he walked he occasionally glanced at letters he was familiar with, naming them in low tones. Each time he did this his step quickened. When he was home he sat down and spread the paper on the ground in the fading afternoon light. It was true: there were plenty of letters like the ones Marie had been showing him. On every line, and often quite close to each other. All those letters cramped up so close! He could hardly believe it! He laughed silently.

Night took him by surprise. That was another of the strange things that had been happening to him these last few days. He went to bed without eating or drinking, leaving the paper on the low shelf that extended from the foot of his bed. It was the first thing he saw next morning. The letters leaped from the paper to his eyes, and he read them out loud.

Even his voice, and the deliberate, clear, precise sounds it made, astonished him. He stopped reading. For a time he just sat on the bed cover and listened to the cawing of the ravens. Then he began again: "*a . . . a . . . a . . . e . . . i . . . a . . . e . . . e . . .*" and so on. He left the cabin and went down to the beach, inhaling the tangy scent, the smell of soil and seaweed that rises at low tide to mingle with the burnt smell of sage from the shoreline.

Two gulls were haggling noisily over something on a rock. All but the end of his dam was high and dry. In the shallow water at the tip herring were milling wildly. Unless all that snakelike threshing meant a sturgeon, or perhaps an eel. Gulls perched attentively on the tall stakes that marked his line of fascines, their heads cocked as they watched for fish, but wary of the turbulence below. Sooner or later, though, they would gather up their courage and devour everything. He should really go down and empty the dam. But he didn't. He let time slip by. He needed nothing; he was happy, with a new indolence, a new sense of ease. For the first time in his life Pierre gazed at the evidence of a good catch without making a move.

No fish lives longer out of water than the sturgeon. An hour sometimes, maybe two. . . . Pierre had often skinned them. You hang the sturgeon head down, tied very tight, from a tree. First you make a cut in the skin all round the base of his tail, then you pull it downward like a sock. As the skin peels away, pink flesh appears. It's hard: you have to tug with all your might. When it's all the way down, like a big empty sausage skin, you cut the head off at the end. And Pierre had seen sturgeon that would leap and fight after that, flopping around on the end of that rope, without a head and without a skin!

Was that a sturgeon in the pen?

Pierre didn't care: the very first letter was *A.* He already knew that yesterday. He'd known for a long time. Everyone knows that the first letter is *A.* He'd picked up a lot from the radio. . . . But today he knew the exact shape of *A.* It had three different shapes, and he knew them all. Pierre squatted down on the beach, and with his hand he cleared a small area of sand near his feet. Then he slowly drew the three shapes in the sand, correcting his too-hasty strokes several times.

He looked at his work and smiled. He had covered the whole space with letters. He wiped it clear again, and this time did *E* and the other vowels. There were lots of other signs on the beach, but they were undisciplined, irregular, littered with pebbles and grit. Birds left tracks on the beach. "But, birds, you can't write! Your tracks mean only that you've been here!" Pierre said aloud. "Nothing else. And then I can come and snare you." But now there was a different set of tracks in front of Pierre—tracks that spoke. He laughed.

Rolling his pants above his knees, he waded onto the mud flat, splashed out to the dam, and peered down to see what was thrashing about so wildly in the water. It was only a big eel. Instantly the gulls flapped in unison into the air.

He realized that he hadn't even brought anything to empty the trap with, and had to return to the cabin for a scoop, a bucket, and a sharp stake. Then he set to work.

He found a few shrimp and ate them, first pinching off their heads. He swallowed the rest, including the shells and the clusters of minute green eggs clinging to the legs.

When he returned to the beach the tide had already turned. The letters on the sand wouldn't last long. He called every one of them by its name, then went back to the cabin.

Pierre removed some small, tender stalks from his bag. They looked like asparagus, with a few wisps of root still clinging to their bases.

"I've brought you some foxtail," he said to Marie.

"What's that?"

"It grows among the stones, by a spring near my place. My mother Nod always kept some, dried. . . ."

"Is it good? It has a thing like a bud on the end there."

"It's good, and it's very bad. It's dangerous. You said, 'I'd prefer dangerous ones, just to see.' That's why I brought this."

"Tell me about it! I love it."

"If you peel it with a knife, you can eat the inside. But only in spring; now, when it's still tender, it's good. If you let it dry, you have to boil it. Then you drink the water. And you get very sick. You hurt all over, but mostly in your stomach. It gets rid of everything you've eaten. It's a purge."

"Oh, how wonderful!" Marie was delighted. She held one of the tiny stalks upright. It was divided into sections by knots, like a miniature bamboo. She twirled it round. "Oh, boy, what I could do with this! It makes me laugh just to think of it! Incredible! You're terrific, Pierre. . . . But it *is* good to eat when it's fresh?" she asked.

"Yes. The Indians used to eat it when they had nothing else. But it's also used for other things."

"Like what?" asked Marie.

"Like . . ." He gazed past her. "My mother Nod said they gave some to her mother, to make my mother Nod come out of her belly. And her mother was very sick. But my mother Nod didn't come out: she went on growing till she was born, and her brothers were angry." Pierre looked at Marie and smiled. "So you see, maybe it's not as bad as they say."

"It doesn't matter," said Marie, then added after a pause, "I wish you would tell me about your mother. Was she really Indian?"

"Only half. The other half was Innuit, Eskimo."

"Well, go on! Tell me more! We can work later, and I have a surprise for you, too. But tell me about your mother first. I swear you don't look like an Eskimo!"

Pierre closed his bag and laid the foxtail roots on the ground. He was absorbed in the task of lining up the stalks. Then, without looking at her, he said, "My mother and my father were not buried. If you're not buried, you're not dead. My mother Nod said so many times."

"Really?"

"She said that then a warrior will wander for ever, down in the bog in the depths of the forest, or up in the Chikchok mountains south of here. The unburied gather there every winter. In summer they go to the mud flats by the shore. Sometimes when I wake up at night I go and listen near the mud flats. They're full of souls seeking rest. But I never hear them. Anyway, I think of my parents then."

"And you're sad. Like me; I'm sad too. But I didn't know. It's a beautiful legend! If I wake up, I'll go and look by the cliff. There's a small mud flat just in front of the house down there. I'll think of my parents and of you, too."

"My father used to laugh and say that they were Innuit and Montagnais stories. He would say that Seal's Blood was speaking through my mother's mouth. Then my mother would get angry and spit on the floor, and my father would stop."

"Who is Seal's Blood?"

"That's my mother Nod's other name. The name she was given when she lived on the reservation. It was my father who called her Nod. Maybe because she didn't like her real name, Seal's Blood."

"Well, I don't like my name either. Marie!"

"Marie is beautiful!"

"No, it isn't. It's *their* name. Maybe I have another name, too, like your mother."

This time Pierre didn't know what to say. He was looking at Marie. The expression in her eyes had changed to one of sadness. She was breathing slowly through her half-open mouth; he could clearly hear the soft whisper of air between the two rows of small teeth. Only their edges were visible, like two very straight lines bordered by the delicate lips. Almost imperceptibly, her mouth closed and she breathed out through her nose, nostrils quivering; she cleared her throat slightly and her lips parted again as she breathed in. Pierre thought that La Noire was a pretty name, too. He remembered the first time they had met, when she said: "My name isn't La Noire!"

Pierre continued with his story, trying to remember everything for Marie. He tried to remember, right from the beginning, from the reservation. His mother, Nod, told him about it many times.

Every year between August and September the Montagnais people journeyed inland to hunt furs. Men, women, and children, everyone but a few old people. They all left the reservation on the coast and traveled deep into the country that white men (so people say) call The Land of Cain. They journeyed toward the tundra, toward game. They wandered very far, covering vast distances, and they did not return for seven months. Perhaps a few might come back down in midwinter if they were short of food, or if they had a corpse to bury—a child, most often, its flesh frozen blue. The rest of the tribe went on.

Ragged and noisy, they laughed constantly and at everything—at the smallest misadventure, at the smallest drama, at their hunting, at their wounds, at their loves. Often the group stretched out in a long line from one horizon to the other, like an endless earthworm cut into sections but still crawling. Sometimes they met a lone Nascuapi hunter, one of the Innuit who roam far south to hunt seal. Then they would compare sleds—the *komatik* hauled by the Indians, and the long sled of the Eskimo. The dogs howled in fury and some of them fought to the death if they were not separated. But the Indians only laughed again, because something had happened.

One year, one of these Nascuapi attached himself to the group. They had seen him coming, waving his arms, from a great way off. He had a magnificent spear with which he killed seal with one sharp blow in the back of the neck. He spoke Montagnais. He was unmarried. He chose a woman and made love to her. One night the brother of this woman took the spear and killed the Nascuapi as he slept, with one sharp blow in the back of the neck. All next day the woman wailed at his side. She did not wish to leave the bloodless corpse lying out on the tundra. But her brother dragged her away. Nod used to say she knew the Nascuapi was not dead. He walked the mud flats and the mountain and the swamp bottoms, seeking her mother's brother.

Nod was born on the reservation the following August. The Indians called her Seal's Blood in mockery of the Nascuapi, the eater of seal blubber. Mother and daughter never again went on the hunt. The people would not let them. They were bearers of bad luck. So they spent their winters with the old and the sick beside the icebergs and the currents of the gulf, under the sun and the long-awaited south wind. The mother brooded and made wide detours to avoid the burial ground. And Seal's Blood grew. She had long black hair, which she tied in a bun with a thong.

That was how he saw her. One winter, when he had already caught a good supply of mink and marten. He had come far, from much farther than the south, from a country that none knew. His hair was as red as flaming heather.

He stopped his *komatik* at the reservation, talked to the old men, and rested. Seal's Blood was fourteen, perhaps fifteen. She prowled around him, his dog, his sled, longing to touch everything.

He knew the Montagnais well; he knew their customs and a little of their language. He spoke to the mother, and they both laughed. But he knew that it would not be simple. That despite their easy palavers, and laughter, and gifts, he would have to put a healthy distance between himself and them. And have a good gun, just in case.

He gave everything he had to the girl: a knife, sugar. He put new moccasins on her feet; and when the old people, drowsy with herbs, had told him part of her story, he also gave her a name. "I will call you Nod," he said. "Get on the sled."

The dog, the man with hair of blazing heather, and Seal's Blood, who sat in the rear of the *komatik*, went west, then south toward the lowest stretches of Bas-du-Fleuve, in search of a safe ice crossing. If there was one.

"Winter on the gulf, January, that's the worst time," said Pierre, digressing from the story. "Because then there's *frasil*."

"What's that?" said Marie.

"Slush ice. Not water, not ice, not snow. Neither solid nor liquid. You can't cross in a boat or on a sled or in snowshoes. You just sink in. If you take a boat, it sticks to the hull, hems you in, and stops you moving. If you come across *frasil,* you have to get away fast! It stretches as far as you can see. Turn back the way you came. You have to escape. Sometimes sailors manage to get through it, because they have big boats and there are many of them to shove and heave and pull on the oars together. But they don't often try. I've been in *frasil* two or three times, and I was lucky to escape every time."

One winter he, Pierre, had stayed longer than usual on the Iles-aux-Ours because hunting had been good. He had found black mink, and six fine green pelts were piled up in the bottom of his sled. On his return journey the *frasil* barrier was slowly setting in. It had almost completely cut his route to Bas-du-Fleuve. Its surface was darker than normal ice and mottled with huge, sinister, greenish reflections. It stretched farther than he could see in the direction of Baie-des-Epaulards.

He had been forced to drag his sled far out into the bay, sweating with the effort. It took him ten hours to cover the familiar route that usually took only three or four. By making a wide detour, he managed to work his way around the edge of the barrier. But even though he was extremely careful, he was unable to avoid slipping into it several times.

He finally reached firm ice high up in the bay. It took another two hours to come down again along the shoreline, and he reached his cabin dead tired. His only food had been a piece of seal hide that he had chewed and chewed. He remained in bed for two days. Pierre's eyes were hundreds of miles away as he recalled the episode. Marie listened, fascinated.

"There were dozens of seal playing out on the gulf. The mothers picked up their pups in their mouths and threw them along the ice. They were sliding and diving. Playing, you know. I passed close by. I didn't have time to hunt them, and they knew it. That's why they were playing. They know everything."

"Oh, boy! You do such interesting things," Marie said.

Pierre smiled and went on with his story.

Some winters strange, sinister things happen. Like that winter. The cold never really settled in. Sudden gusts of warm air blew up unexpectedly. The ice was streaked with shifting colors. It turned green and soft under the mild, caressing west winds that blew off the land. You would have thought it was the spring thaw, except that this was January. The next day the *nordet,* the icy north wind, shrilled again around the screams of the gulls, and pack ice stiffened once more and bit into the land. The *nordet* always blows for three days, not a day less. After it dropped, a snowstorm raged for a week. Then one morning the sky reappeared, drained of its last snowflake, and so blue its light hurt Pierre's eyes. You had to look at the earth and the trees or else go blind. In the evening the sun set in the northwest like a fireball slowly dropping from the never-ending blue, dipping into the gulf ice like a curved axe blade. Everything bled. The chaos of huge bergs glittered with red coals, diamonds, emeralds, and sapphires.

Sometimes wolves crossed the whole breadth of the bay at night. They came from the north, from the far shore, from beyond the Iles, lured perhaps by vague, disturbing smells borne over vast distances by the careening winds. You could hear them howling their hunger. And then, next day, everything foundered again. Currents swirled in the bay and the gulf; rapids foamed between bergs floating free among seal and patches of *frasil*; snow squalls raged around pillars of living ice; snowdrifts piled up, big as dunes and bristling with black bush-pine trunks that thrust out at all angles to the white, white, white horizons around them. It was breathtaking. "And that's how it was, too, when my father and my mother Nod crossed the gulf," Pierre said.

To Pierre's father, the crossing had looked feasible from the Iles-aux-Ours. The channels were closed and frozen solid. They had gone out onto the ice. Little Nod got out of the sled and helped heave on the harness already drawn taut by the dog, both of them floundering on the slippery surface. Pierre's father had known that, once they were on the other side, no one would come for them, and if they did, he would be waiting. They reached Baie-des-Epaulards. The cabin was no more than a rough shelter, and they both set to work enlarging it. Two years later Pierre was born.

Marie said, "Then you spoke Indian with your mother?"

"Yes, a little. When I was very young I remember my parents spoke to each other in the language of the Montagnais. So did I. But as I grew up I began to speak both languages, and so did my mother Nod. Then, after I was alone, I almost forgot Montagnais. I spoke only with the people around here, the village fishermen, if they came; hunters, the Voyageur, campers. . . ."

66

"Say something in Indian."

"What?"

"Anything. Whatever you like."

"*Quâ-quâ sut!*"

"That sounds funny! What does it mean?"

"'Forest devil.' You know, wolverine. The Indians all hate him."

"Why?"

"He wrecks everything he finds. He eats everything. He springs your traps. He's cleverer than any hunter, he kills whatever he wants. And he eats! He eats and he eats. That's why he's called a glutton as well. He can even take on a caribou. And when he's had enough he spoils the rest: he dirties it."

"He must be crazy!"

"*Quâ-quâ sut!* Luckily there aren't too many round here. I've killed one, just one," Pierre said.

"So!"

"Aren't you going to say anything? I killed a wolverine!"

"Maybe you were right. If it's true he's so bad," said Marie.

"Teach me some more letters," said Pierre.

"Wait a minute. Look what I have here. Paper, a notebook, two pencils. Anyway, one pencil with lead; I hope you can sharpen it with your knife. The other writes with ink; there's enough in it for a long time. Do you like them?"

"Thank you. You know, I've already seen things like that—those pens and pencils."

"Now you can practice writing all the letters I teach you. You have to. And syllables and sounds. All of them. And that's why you need the paper, so you can read them and copy them over and over, as many times as you can. To practice."

"And if the pencils wear out, I'll get others from the Voyageur."

"Oh, I'll give you others. But you can begin with these."

He held the notebooks and pencils like an offering in front of him, his rough hands gently caressing them.

"Come on, have a try. Start with the vowels, okay?" Marie said.

She helped him set the book across his knees and then showed him how to hold the pencil properly. She pointed to the top of the first page, and he started writing. Clumsily, he made a capital *A,* then the two small ones.

She couldn't take her eyes off the page. Wordlessly he went on with the other vowels.

"Why, you're really talented. That's fantastic."

"I wrote them before. On the sand. At my place."

"So!"

"So!" He laughed; his head was thrown back and his blue eyes flashed a happiness like that of a triumphant child.

Marie sat down again. "All right now, listen," she said. "You have to fill out one line with each letter, right? So that you learn how to draw them properly. The more letters you draw, the better you'll get."

"The sooner I'll be able to write," said Pierre.

He made himself more comfortable and gripped the pencil firmly, trying out several positions with his fingers. Gradually, as he moved to the right across the page, he mastered *e.* When he reached the end of the line, he began the next with *i*. The dot seemed too faint, so he pressed down and made it too big.

"You need an eraser," Marie said. "How dumb I am! I'll steal one from him, he has loads. But I'll get you something better than this. I'll get you a special book, one with blank pages next to pages with the letters all written out and ready to be copied. When you've filled the whole book, you'll be able to write."

"And read?"

"Of course. I was keeping it as a surprise, but you write so well I can't keep it a secret anymore. . . . But be patient, you'll see. We'll be going down to the village one of these days and I'll get everything you need: notebooks, textbooks, everything."

"It'll take a long time," said Pierre. "Will you be here?"

"Every afternoon, if you like."

She was pale, and he could see the blood moving under the skin of her cheeks and neck. She would come here every day and teach him all the letters. Pierre smiled, and his eyes stayed on Marie; he couldn't move. He watched her, pencil in hand. "You're so small," he said at last. "You never stop moving. Like a raccoon's face." She burst out laughing.

"Hey, you!"

"That's right," he said. "A little she-raccoon. Very small and very busy. They never slow down. Even down in their burrows their faces go on twitching. All through February, every night, they stay underground and wait for their mates to come home."

"He says I'm ugly because of my ears. Did you notice? One's bigger than the other."

69

"Yes."

"But if I hide part of it with my hair, and you don't look me straight in the face, you don't realize."

"Yes, I do."

"Oh."

"Just like a she-raccoon. And up above, the male hustles around all night long, turning over everything he finds and poking his nose into tree holes and snow caves. In the morning he goes back home. She-raccoons are beautiful, you know."

So Pierre and Marie met every day. Near the big
white house, in the clearing formed by the big gray
boulders that stood crookedly in the grass and sand.
The clearing was enclosed on three sides by this de-
bris from a long-forgotten landslide. On the fourth
side were trees—cedar, aspen, hazel—and through
the branches you could see the flat expanse of the gulf
stretching to the horizon. On a clear day you could see
part of the forest on the Iles-aux-Ours.

No one could see them in this rockbound scallop.
You would have had to slip through the narrow passage, as they did, or else approach from the shore
below the trees. But the slope plunged steeply amid
tree trunks and underbrush, and they would have
heard. Pierre could escape down the slopes if he

needed to; he could follow the shore right round the headland and get away, as Marie had said.

Often he arrived by the Cape road, and she would be waiting for him near the fence in front of the white house. She would wave while he was still far off. Then they would skirt the wooded property together and slip behind the rocks.

On other days, like today, he took the lower road, by the water, slowly climbed the slope and emerged in the middle of the clearing.

In his bag was the notebook in which he practiced writing, pencils, an eraser, a spelling book, and also that book Marie had promised him, with blank lines to fill with letters and sounds and maybe even words. Will it be soon? he wondered. One time when he had opened his bag, Marie had said, "At least you look like a student and not a savage." She had been pleased with him.

Pierre put his things down near a small sumac and waited. Then he changed his mind and went to see if Marie was waiting by the fence. She wasn't.

He returned to the rocks and sat down.

Long wisps of mist floated low among the branches. Sometimes they masked whole stretches of the gulf, then slowly dispersed and re-formed farther on. Pierre's eyes followed the white, curling, vaporous tendrils as they sank to the ground and clung to the grass. The damp lacework of ferns sparkled under the delicate, ephemeral crystals.

A foghorn had been moaning regularly since morning. Perhaps its automatic system had been upset by the intermittent onslaught of dense fog patches that swirled away, just as suddenly as they had arrived, revealing a clear blue sky. An hour later they were back again. Pierre sat and waited. The damp branches of a massive oak exhaled a smell of leather.

There weren't many blank pages left in the notebook. It was filling up with lines of writing. As he progressed through the book, Pierre's lettering was not only steadily shrinking in size, but was taking on a firmer shape.

Marie checked his work each day, leafing through the book and making corrections. Then she worked out a new exercise for him, tapping her teeth with a pencil as she pondered. One time, Pierre remembered, she had said, "Right. Today you can do this. Here, read it. Good. . . . Make two whole lines. And say it out loud while you're writing. Don't forget . . . you're going to look silly talking to yourself. Anyway, you told me you talk to yourself, so . . . And lower down, you can write what we're going to study now. We can put the book away for the moment. I like your birch bag."

"You can have it."

"What next?"

"I can make one for you. A new one, if you like."

"No. Thank you, Pierre, but I don't think you should. She'd say it was ugly or something. She'd throw it away for no reason; she'd burn it. And I'd be unhappy, because then when I think of you, I'll get mad. Throwing things away is what she likes best. Everything she lays her hands on. She even throws away stuff she bought herself if she's in the mood. He's the opposite. He holds on to all kinds of rubbish.

She says, 'Why, I got rid of it, no one was using it!' Then he gets mad and they start all over again. No, you keep the bag. I'd rather not."

Pierre recalled the time when he had first seen Marie. She was crying. The sobs were shaking her whole body. She tried to hold them back, she kept blinking to stop the tears. Then she wiped them away with her hand.

At first he had thought her parents had beaten her, the way his father sometimes beat him. But she had said it was nothing. She was far from the house, there was no one around. No one. So why?

And where could she be now? Pierre wondered.

He thought of taking a look round the house. Without going in. Quietly. He could listen.

The hot, damp afternoon dragged on. Dogs were barking in the distance.

Marie had never been so late. Maybe they've left, he thought, his body suddenly tense. Was the car outside the house? Pierre couldn't contain himself any longer. He slipped between the rocks, came out into the open, and looked around.

There was no sound, and nothing was moving around the house.

He returned to the rock clearing and sat down again. He waited some more. He was hot, and his shirt was sticking to his skin. He unbuttoned the neck and began to think of Marie again.

"They have asphalt streets," she had said another time. "Lots of streets. A city, for heaven's sake! And cars everywhere. And lots of skyscrapers, all huddled up together. When you look up, you can hardly see

74

the sky. My poor Pierre, there aren't even any birds:
just a few small trees in a little park. Ridiculous! And
you'd like to go there? You don't know how lucky you
are! This is the only good part of the year, when we
come here in summer. The rest of the time it's sub-
ways, monorails, buses, and yukkh! So!"

"I'd like to see a train," he had said then.

"What?"

"A train, you know, that goes on rails. I've heard a
lot about them. I saw a photograph of one in a
paper. . . . Lots of photographs. As big as a house,
right?"

"Let's not exaggerate. A little house. The locomotive, maybe. . . . And the cars too, I suppose. . . . So
you've never seen a train! That's just incredible. But
you're right, I guess, the nearest line is two villages
from here. A train! Why? Trains are a bore. I think
so, anyway."

"But they're big and they travel fast, you could go
down the whole coast in just a few hours. Some campers told me once. They told me all about trains. They
were kids with motorbikes, they were making fun of
me, they'd come on the train to get here quicker.
They'd put their motorbikes on the train! They carry
automobiles, too, you know. They must be as big as
your house! A whole line of cars hooked together, and
the locomotive up front, hauling all the rest. I understood the whole thing. . . ."

"So?"

"How do they work?"

"It's hard to explain, Pierre. By electricity. It
makes the wheels go round."

75

"I could walk as far as the track. I've wanted to go for a long time. But I never got round to it."

"Well, you were quite right. It's kid stuff." She was laughing, Pierre remembered. Yes, Marie was laughing and flicking little pebbles at him with her thumbnail.

"I know, I'll teach you my stone game! First you lay them out in three rows. . . . Oh, no, you have to be able to add and everything. Boy, am I dumb. I'm going to have to teach you arithmetic as well. We have an awfully long way to go."

"Teach me some more letters."

She had to teach him some more letters. There were still lots to go. "An incredible number," she had said. Maybe Marie had been crying because she was lonely. Did she often cry? But she had said, "I like when there's no one around, there's nothing I like better, there's no one to bother you." Pierre's thoughts were now beginning to jump from one episode to another, but always, always in the end he wondered why Marie had been crying.

The light was already fading. The whitish humidity of day was taking on the blues and grays of twilight, and still Marie had not come. Pierre was afraid to go anywhere or do anything. The nearby house was silent; all he could hear from that direction was the chatter of a flock of redbreasts, noisily celebrating their newfound home in a wild cherry tree. Their presence only confirmed that the house was deserted.

He listened. The foghorn blared obsessively, gulls squawked from time to time, a chipmunk chattered as it bustled from tree to tree. He looked. The fog was thickening as the tide came in at the foot of the Cape. Pine and birch tops were disappearing in the mist, and down on the ground the rocks were damp under their spotty coating of red lichen.

He got up and left.

Pierre felt restless. He carried wood to the cabin and ate some vegetables he had cooked the day before. He turned on the radio and listened absently to the words and music, but he could not picture what he heard, as he usually could. Static from distant storms crackled in the set. He picked out a man's voice saying that the heat wave would last several days. He turned the set off.

He lit a candle and began to write. He said out loud what he had learned the day before, slowly, and his handwriting was firm, but soon he was bored, and stopped. He got up. Finally he lay down and went to sleep.

Next morning the mist had turned to pea soup. The trees near the white-blanketed cabin were barely visible. You only sensed the pine trunks and the shape of the bushes. You sometimes get days like this in the middle of summer, days that suddenly shut themselves in, in a kind of gloomy expectation, wrapped in silence, without even a bird call, heavy with the smell of seaweed. Nothing seems to stir anywhere: the world is reduced to a circle a few steps wide; everything else is cocooned in mystery. Movement seems pointless and out of place. One thought fills a whole hour. It is hot, but you think you are cold. Because of the strangeness. You know the tide is in, but there are no waves and no splashing; only the slack smell of water and iodine mingled with fish.

Pierre walked to the path and was soon under the high trees. He walked for a long time, thinking of Marie, wondering where she was. She had said, "Learning to read takes time." He knew that. Leaving the pine forest, he reached a small stream and the beaver dam. Hanging in a snare on the end of a springy branch was a beaver.

He untied the animal, dropped it on the ground, and began to reset the snare. With nimble fingers he set out the bait, a young sprig of willow with small, still-fresh rootlets clinging to it. It would be even better bait now that it had the smell of beaver on it. He tied the delicacy behind the wire noose, then fixed them both to the flexible branch which was held down by a forked stick. Finally he pinned the noose to the ground with a wooden hook which he pressed gently into the grass along the narrow track the animal would be taking. When it snared itself in the noose, it would tear the whole contraption loose, and the branch would whip upward and hoist the beaver out of reach of thieves.

Once he had set the snare, Pierre examined the beaver. Its pelt was superb after the April molt. It was about six months old, he guessed. And he was a male: Pierre thought of rubbing the beaver's glands over the bait. Then the trap would be deadly. But he took the beaver and left.

Pierre had an idea. With a beaver, he could walk right up to the white house. He'd knock at the door.

Marie would open it, she'd say good morning, but he wouldn't show the beaver.

Or else they'd open the door. Him or her? Then he'd show the beaver. But Marie had said, "You mustn't sell them anything."

Then she might come out and see the beaver. She had said, "Couldn't your father have taught you other things? So!" And, "You're bad."

"But I didn't know," Pierre said aloud. "I know now."

He could say it was an old pelt from last year. "It's a fresh one." That's what she'd say.

Then he would admit it. He'd found it in a trap this morning. So he took it. If you leave a dead beaver near a dam, all the others panic and leave. It's a male, and it smells. "Who set the trap? So!" would be Marie's reply.

But he'd see Marie. Why didn't she come yesterday? Where is she? he thought as he had done a hundred times since the day before. And what if she said, "How disgusting!" What if she were angry?

And the missing letters? Learning to read takes time. Pierre couldn't stop thinking of Marie. Perhaps she went to the village, or even farther; she should certainly be back soon. When? He would go back to the white house, he would sit down, and he would wait, that was all.

He went to the beach near his cabin, rolled up his pant legs, and sat down with his feet in the water to skin the beaver.

He kept the four glands—the two juicy ones, and the two deeper-lying ones whose oil is so good for baiting traps and snares.

Then he removed the skin with a knife-point. He kept the good pieces of meat and threw the carcass and entrails into the sea. Gulls had already emerged from the fog, attracted by a smell that they alone could detect, and had started to squabble even before they had sufficient courage to swoop down on the red-stained water around Pierre.

He washed the pelt and hung it on a branch near the cabin. He looked at the pelt and wondered if Marie was right. Was he bad?

He prowled around restlessly. Then he went inside, took the bag containing his books, the notebook and pencils, and left for the Cape.

There was no one at the white house.

He reached the clearing among the rocks, sat down, and waited as he had done the day before. He sat mindlessly in the enveloping fog.

The damp summer closed in all round him. His head nodding, his eyelids growing heavy in the moist heat, he listened to the deep sound of his own breathing. Little by little he stretched out on the sparse grass and sand of the clearing, his trunk and limbs settling into the horizontal almost without knowing it. He fell asleep, and did not hear Marie when she arrived. She was smiling; her features were veiled by the mist floating in her hair. She leaned over him. He opened his eyes. There was nobody there. Just a small, broken wormwood sprig, dangling sheepishly, its dried berries hanging in dusty little clusters. A flat rock face blocking his view. Nobody. Heat, and the sugary scent of sage brush.

Slowly he got to his knees; they sank into the

ground a little. He took his knife from his pocket and opened it. Its point was very sharp. He went to the rock and began to carve with great care. The last letter he had learned, and all the things it could say when you added vowels to it. After a very long time, the rock face said to Marie: FA FE FI FO FOU FAU FEU FAI.

He left at low tide. The Cape was alive with muffled noises and muffled voices. The cawing of crows rang over the heat-prostrated *savane*. In the distance the forest, too, slept in the heat, the aspen leaves dropped, the grass was turning yellow. The evening sun broke through the mist with difficulty, a pale orange ball, infinitely distant, imperceptibly revolving.

Back in his cabin Pierre looked at the log walls. One year, the year when seal pelts sold so well, his father had bought pine planks and nailed them to the logs. The vertical rows covered two whole walls. His father had also built a shelf that was now heaped with hunting gear, cooking pots, and candles. Another year Pierre had finished the job by adding more shelves, with hooks beneath them to hang his clothes. But there was still a lot more room on the plank wall at the foot of the bed, and as he looked at it Pierre had an idea.

He spread some newspapers on the table, examined them, and then began to cut out letters. All the letters that said anything. Then he sorted them. There were big printing characters, complete syllables, sometimes even a word—everything that Pierre recognized. He heated the glue he used for his harpoons and began to stick the letters on the plank wall.

He arranged identical letters side by side, then moved to more complex sounds, close together the way he had written them in his notebook. There were many of them, and they took up a huge space on the wall.

It took time. When he had finished he looked. There was still a lot of pale, blank, silent wood left. When would it be filled up? he agonized. Where was Marie?

Next day the mist had gone. Everything grilled under the sun. The bay was drowned in a harsh glare. Bird calls woke Pierre and he left his cabin. He ate sitting outside, with the gulf stretching before him.

The tide was turning, setting up long ripples on the surface, liquid wrinkles that seemed to generate spontaneously on the shoreline and which slowly retreated seaward. A little farther out all movement was lost in the flat, smooth brilliance of the water. Beyond were zones of varied colors, stretches of green so dark it was almost black, long shadows marking undersea deeps. Pierre recognized some of them. Gulls made small pinpoints on the surface. Still farther out all details were lost in the infinite reaches of water where porpoise rolled and flashed. And on the outer horizon lay the long, low, dark shapes of the Iles, four or five shadowy silhouettes trembling in the haze. It took four hours of steady walking to reach them across the ice in winter. Behind the Iles was infinity, under a white, motionless sky. You couldn't see the opposite shore. Yet Pierre knew that beyond those wild lands, beyond that yawning horizon, there was as much water again—another immense, shifting wasteland—

before you reached the other side of the gulf and his mother's land. Everything was swallowed up in space. The unusual absence of wind intensified the calm of this hot, blue morning. Flying low in the sky, a flock of bustard seemed one with eternity, endlessly winging eastward over the open sea, diminishing slowly into the distance, and leaving an unanswered question behind them.

"I didn't want to go, I tell you, Pierre, I didn't want to go! But they'd made up their minds to visit friends. They called them: 'We're getting bored here.' (They get bored all the time.) So off we went with the suit-cases and the car and the lot. Their friends are idiots. They talk like the TV, they repeat everything they hear, like parrots. They tell jokes everyone knows. You can't imagine. . . ." She broke off with a sigh.

"I didn't want to go, but he did," she continued. "So he beat me. I don't care. He thinks it hurts, and she thinks it's very good for your education. But it doesn't worry me; it doesn't hurt. I decided to go, so it would look as if I was being obedient, but really I thought, if I go, I'll find a way to buy more books for you. For our lessons and for later when you can read. So.

"And that's what I did," she went on. "It's only a small town, but it has a great bookshop. Naturally, at their friends' place they talked and told jokes and ate and drank and their eyes turned small the way they do when they're drunk. Then they said they were tired. I went up to bed. I was the only one up next morning, I took some money from his coat pocket and went into town and bought all the things you need. Look: five books, good ones, you'll see. I got this, too, it's a present. It's a fountain pen, and here's a bottle of ink to fill it. Look, this is how."

The books were colored. Pierre opened them. They were full of letters, words, photographs, and drawings. He didn't know where to begin. He closed them, and watched Marie as she filled the pen and explained to him.

"There, did you see? There's enough ink in it for a long time. Do you like it?"

Pierre laughed. Marie was back. She is very pale, he thought, looking at her, and her hair is black.

"I was very quick," she said. "I went back home and hid them in my suitcase. They were still asleep. The only good thing at their friends' place is the cat. I gave him milk and combed his fur and he rubbed against me. Then we had breakfast. I was still thinking about you, I couldn't wait to see you. Just waiting for them to make up their minds to leave! Maybe we would be in time for me to see you in the afternoon. Next time I'll leave a signal for you, a piece of paper or something. That'll mean, 'Wait, I've gone away, but I'll be back.' We should've thought of it before! But when we got back it was too late, it was almost evening. I came anyway, but you weren't there. But I saw your letters. So."

"I didn't know what to do," said Pierre.

"They look nice on the rock."

"Are there many more letters?"

"Oh, yes. But we'll learn them quickly. You've made a good start, you understand everything so far. You're very intelligent, Pierre! Don't be sad. Trust me. You'll see."

"Television must be nice."

"And anyway, there aren't that many letters left. Now it's mainly putting them in groups. Lots of them are long. But you'll be surprised, you'll see. . . . Television?" said Marie. "Haven't you ever seen it?"

"Yes, once, at the campsite. There was a man there with a big house on wheels. He had television."

"That's right, they put in electricity down there."

"Well, I was hiding in the trees at the back. Then I came nearer and no one said anything. I saw it clearly. It was a game of ball."

"Football."

"Yes. I watched for a long time. I could see it all, but I couldn't hear much."

"And you liked it?"

"Yes."

"Well, that's okay. Because you never see anything out in the woods there. But you'd soon get tired of television. One day, if they go out, I'll take you into the house and show you. But not football. I can't stand football. . . . Listen, do you want to work, or what?"

"Yes," said Pierre.

"All right, open your notebook and give it to me. We'll look at one of the new books later. You'll see, it's just the same as your notebook. But we have to start with that." She reviewed his work, then turned to the next page and said, "See, look, here's the G. And that one, and that one, for reading and for writing. Now try to copy them. And don't get it mixed up with C, okay? Be careful. . . ."

She watched in silence as Pierre wrote. After a moment she said, "Make two lines as usual, all right?"

He stopped writing and looked up at her. "If he beat you, he must be bad," he said.

"Of course. What did you think?"

"Then why did she say it's good for your education?"

"Listen, you make everything complicated. That's just what they always say: it's good for children's education. She beats me, too, you know."

"Sometimes my father used to beat me."

"They tell lies all the time. It's no good trying to understand. Later you'll read books, then you'll understand."

"So did my mother Nod. She beat me, too, sometimes. Do they teach you that it's right in books?"

"No, no! But you get to understand everything. Everything is in books, I tell you. They do it because they're ignorant. So. If they learned, can you imagine how they would be? No, you can't imagine it, because you can't read yet. But when you can, you will—and then you'll understand what I mean. You'll see that you know nothing, and then you'll want to learn. You have to begin at the beginning. It's the best way." She stopped as he was still looking at her. "Have you finished?" she asked.

"No."

"Then go on. . . . Listen," she said. "They can read, naturally. But they don't read to learn. What they read is all wrong: garbage, stupid things. As soon as it begins to teach them something they get bored. And they think they know! But they know even less than you. They're always going on about something, the problems of mankind. 'We're living in dangerous times, the bourgeoisie understands nothing about art, world poverty.' . . . They'll talk about anything. But they do nothing! And that's because they don't care about the main thing. So! The main thing is to learn, not to recite! When you read, you're happy. Everything seems beautiful. When you can read you'll know what it's like to float up to heaven and be as light as a bird." She was smiling now.

"You'll open a book and you'll read this," she went on without giving Pierre a chance to say something. "Listen, I know the beginning by heart: 'Tell me, Muse, of the man of many wiles' . . . and after that you won't be able to stop. You'll read pages and pages of fantastic adventures. They'll make your hair stand on end, they'll make you shiver, you wait! Then you'll open another, and it'll be the same: you'll be flying. There's nothing like it. . . . Have you finished?" she asked.

Pierre handed her the notebook. He had finished the two lines of letters and begun a third with the letters GA.

"That's it," said Marie. "You've got it, it'll come quickly now, I promise."

"If we go into the white house one day," said Pierre, "could I speak on the telephone?"

"Why?"

"I never have."

"That's amazing."

"I'd like to."

"It's true, I guess, since you don't know anyone outside here. You're just like a child! Okay, if you like I'll take you into the house one day when they're away, and you can watch television and talk on the telephone. So. I can't call long distance, though, because they'd find out and there'd be questions and everything, but . . . Anyway, back to work," she said. "Write the next letter."

"The sailbirds came this morning," he said as he began to fill a line with the letter *H*.

"What are they?"

"Small birds, tiny birds. When a whole flock flies together, it's like a sail swelling and flapping in the wind. They always fly in very tight groups, and they all land at once on the beach or the mud flats. Like a sail coming down. . . . They came this morning."

Pierre stopped talking. He was suddenly sad. Marie looked at him in surprise.

"If you let your mind wander like this, you'll never learn," she said. "I hope you aren't going to shoot the sailbirds?"

"You can't kill sailbirds," said Pierre. "They're too small and they're no good for anything. I haven't killed a single bird this summer. Since you told me. Nothing else, either."

"And the beaver you told me about?... Before I could say anything, you told me all about the beaver."

"That was to give to your parents, and then maybe I could've seen you. But I didn't kill him. That trap's been there for years. He trapped himself."

Marie laughed, and Pierre, too, felt trapped. But he could tell she wasn't very angry about the beaver. He added quickly: "And you know my jackrabbit run? Well, I haven't even laid any bait. Not a jackrabbit in a long time."

"Good, that's fine," said Marie. "Now, come on, we've got to work."

But Pierre's mind was elsewhere.

"Now the sailbirds are here we have no time to lose," he said.

"Why are you going on about sailbirds?"

"When they come," said Pierre, "it means summer will be ending. Bit by bit. The leaves turn red and the water gets muddy. After that everyone leaves the Cape. I won't see you again. And I haven't finished learning to read."

"Oh," said Marie, "so that's what's on your mind. You know we leave last of all, at least a month after the others. So! If you want to, you *will* be able to read. What a baby you are!"

But Pierre continued to feel gloomy. He nodded slightly, took the spelling book and leafed through it to the end. There were still a lot of pages. Marie took it back and said: "There are thirteen more letters, because you already know the vowels and lots of things. And the more you learn the easier it gets from now on."

Pierre said nothing. He sat huddled and unmoving. Marie looked at him.

"I don't think you look well, Pierre," she said. "You look tired."

"No."

"Have you ever been sick?"

"No."

"Thank heaven! What would you do if you were sick, if you had appendicitis? Perhaps you don't eat enough. What did you eat at noon? Just to see."

"At noon? Nothing, because I ate this morning when I came back from getting wood. It was low tide and I emptied my fish trap. Then I ate a herring. So you see . . ."

"Well, at least you didn't eat *that* raw! That's some progress, at least. Without bread?"

"I have bread. I've already told you, bread you can keep for months. And I make bannocks, too. But I don't eat too many."

"Your Indian bread? That's funny. You know, a herring isn't much. I'm hungry, all the time. But you're not. It's strange."

"I ate the herring raw," said Pierre. "What is appendicitis?"

"Don't worry about it. You won't get it. Don't worry, it's very rare. Will you bring me some of your bread one day? Just to see?"

"I'll bring some tomorrow."

"Wonderful! Then I won't worry so much this winter when I think of you. I'll know the way you live, what you eat, everything. The clothes you wear, how you keep warm. I'd like to go to your place some

91

day, too. You might need something, and I could get it for you before I left. . . ." She broke off and her eyes suddenly widened. "A live herring! Ugghh!"

"It's a long way to my place. It's down on the beach behind the little wood. People don't often come because it's so far. Campers sometimes: if I don't bring them fish for a few days, they come. Sometimes hunters and fishermen come, too. They ask me questions and look around. I like to see them and talk to them."

"We could meet at your place!" Marie said. "Tomorrow, if you like, I'll go down the road at the end of the Cape. The road leading down to the *savane*. You can wait for me there and lead me to your cabin."

"Okay," said Pierre.

Marie gave him the book, then counted off on her fingers: "I've given you paper, pencils, the pen. You can already write a little . . . all the syllables I've taught you. You're doing very well. And listen: tomorrow I'll bring you another book, a very, very big book. A dictionary."

"What's that?"

"It has every word in it. Say you're looking for a word . . . 'locomotive,' okay? It tells you how to spell it and explains what it is. Sometimes it has a photo or drawing beside it to show you."

"Every word?"

"Every word. Can you imagine? You can find out every single thing you need to know. And you don't need me or anyone else. You can do it by yourself. So. You want to see a train? You look under *train*. Of course, you have to know how to spell it. . . . Going to see a train! What an idea, you'd die of fright!'

92

"I see airplanes every day. Cars, motorbikes. But no trains."

"Crazy idea. Tomorrow I'll give you the diction-ary. . . . Now listen, I'm going to tell you something. A poem. Do you know what that is?"

"Yes."

"How do you know?"

"They say them on the radio sometimes. They're very beautiful. I never understand much: poems are when people don't speak the way other people speak, or the way I speak. But I like the words. . . . Other times, though, I don't like them so much. I don't know why."

"I'm the same way. They're just words stuck to-gether, and sometimes they don't mean a thing. Don't you mind. I'm the same way. But you'll see, some poems are very clear. Listen, here's one: 'My child, my sister, dream/ How sweet all that would seem/ Were we in that kind land to live together,/ And there love slow and long,/ There live and die among/ Those scenes that image you, that sumptuous weather.' Good, huh? Did you understand?"

"Yes, but you didn't read it. Did you make it up?"

"No. I know it by heart. The beginning anyway. Did you notice? You remember it right away. It's like a song. I'll get poetry books for you to read."

She was silent for a moment, then said: "When you can read you'll never be alone again. So!"

"But I haven't been alone since this summer," said Pierre. "Since I've been meeting you. Every day I wait for noon so I can come here, and in the evening I think of everything you've told me."

"That's just so you can learn to read."

"It's to see you as well."

"Same for me. Instead of walking in the woods or on the beach the way I did other years. I was always alone."

She broke off a small hazel twig—three leaves and a small, withered berry. She put it in her mouth and made a face.

"I have a friend in the city," she said. "We tell each other everything we do and everything we think. She tells me what happened to her at home. And we read the same things. I like her a lot. I know you'd like her, too. And she'd like you! Is she going to ask me some questions! But you know, I don't think I'll be able to tell her everything. Not about you, at least, not everything about you. Naturally, I'll tell her I taught you to read. That'll kill her. Fantastic! But she'll never know who you are. Because you're just for me . . . my secret. Do you understand?"

"You, too," said Pierre. He meant that Marie was his friend, just for him. As if he'd known her a long time. As if she had known his father, and his mother Nod. As if she had lived with them, and then with him after they didn't come back to the cabin. And he wanted to say that he could never tell anyone about Marie, and that he didn't know why she was crying that first day, near the white fence by her garden.

He looked at Marie. She was wearing a brown wool sweater that came down low over her blue pants. She had a very thin silver bracelet, like a rabbit snare, around her wrist. She opened her reading book.

"Tomorrow," said Pierre, "I'm going to give you something, too."

"What?"

"Something to make a jewel with."

"A jewel? Wonderful! What is it?"

"They say it's very beautiful, they keep asking me for one. 'You wouldn't have a tooth, would you, Le Rouge?' That's what they say."

"How stupid! 'Le Rouge,' that annoys me. What kind of tooth?"

"An *épaulard* tooth."

"What's an *épaulard*?"

"Even bigger than a whale. And stronger than whales, because it eats whales."

"I don't believe you."

"Yes, yes, it eats whales, and seals, and birds... everything."

"So that's why people here call this place Orcs Bay! It's an orca—a killer whale. It's not an *épaulard,* this animal!"

"Yes, that's right. One was washed ashore on Iles Vertes one year. He was stranded on the mud flats during the low tides. So the fishermen came and opened him up. You know what they found inside? A baby whale, all chopped up, and more than a dozen seals. Can you believe it? His belly was as big as an automobile!"

"That's a story! You weren't there!"

"But I went to take a look afterward, because the smell reached my beach. Every time the southwester blew there was a smell of rot. The Voyageur told me about it. He said they took ten hours to kill it. Nobody had seen an *épaulard* since the lighthouse went on to automatic and the two keepers killed one. They killed theirs properly! They knew how! But that was seven years ago, and no one could remember how to do it anymore. They pumped bullets into him, the jackasses. And the orca? He just died his own natural death. That's what the Voyageur thought, anyway. And the next day, they started to cut him up. Naturally they didn't tell the cooperative about it—they all wanted a chunk for themselves. Even the seal pelts in his belly, his teeth, everything. They wanted every scrap. It went on for a week. Then the people from the Ministry came. The Voyageur didn't know how they found out. An informer most likely. They took their cut, too—the biggest part, because the people from the village didn't know how to haul it away. 'What they left is what's stinking,' the Voyageur said to me. 'That's what you can smell over here, Le Rouge.'" Pierre made a face.

"I told the Voyageur I would go and look," he went on. "It was completely rotten. I took some of the blubber they'd left. And pulled out a tooth. The carcass stayed there until the ice started to eat it and the thaw took it out to sea. I went back there in spring and there was nothing left."

Marie had been listening to him, fascinated.

"I sometimes see whales in the gulf," she said. "When I can get his binoculars I watch them. But I never see much above the surface. Maybe I've seen an orca without knowing?"

"Yes."

"Are you going to give me his tooth?"

"Yes."

"I love you, Pierre. Do you know?"

"I love you, too," said Pierre.

Marie picked up the notebook and handed it to Pierre. They studied more groups using the letter *h*. Pierre mumbled earnestly to himself, and Marie laughed at his expression as he mouthed the sounds. Then they did a short dictation, using the syllables he had learned.

Next they looked at *j* and *k*. Pierre learned how to pronounce and write them under Marie's supervision. She was amused by his determination to get every upstroke just right. There was even one word, a word Pierre didn't know, that contained both letters. "You can look it up in the dictionary. So!" said Marie.

That day she explained that you could put several sounds together, side by side, and make a complicated word. She showed him examples, putting together vowels and consonants. Following the instructions in the book, she made him pronounce everything out loud before going on. As she watched Pierre's growing amazement she was flooded with warmth and with a fierce joy that impelled her to drive on from one explanation to the next. "You'll see, you'll see," she kept saying excitedly. Pierre's exultation infected her, too, and Marie tried as hard as she could to trip her pupil with questions. But it was no good. Nothing could slow his momentum. It was as if Pierre had suddenly grasped the whole system, after days of barely comprehending its outline—all those disembodied crumbs of sound she had thrown him, sounds he had learned by heart but which seemed to serve no purpose. But now everything held together and made sense. Words! Whole words that he had heard and spoken a thousand times: there they were now, lying right

97

there on the page like animals whose physical components you could understand. Words! Words which spoke!

When they stopped studying, Pierre cut some blades of grass. He laid them out in front of him, at Marie's knees. He arranged them in the shape of letters, and wrote out a word. Marie leaned over and kissed him on the cheek.

Marie was coming down the Cape road. Just where it
turns sharply at the foot of the slope and heads off
through the undergrowth in the direction of Orcs
Bay. It finally reaches the village after disappearing
under high forest, crossing the maple stands and
skirting the rock outcrops that jut over the outlying
houses.

Looking landward, all you can see of this area is
savane and the slopes leading up to the Cape. Toward
the sea are flooded mud flats. Pierre was waiting and
saw Marie emerge from beneath the trees. She
waved. She had the straw bag she sometimes carried
her books in, a blue sweater, blue canvas pants, and
tennis shoes. She had undone her hair, and it blew
around her face in the wind.

Pierre got up from the grass.

Side by side they walked down to the high-water line. Then they walked along the narrow strip of sand where tufts of water barley, stirring in the faintest breeze, bobbed their heads in salute to clumps of fading blue iris. The path between land and water was not wide enough to walk abreast, and Pierre led the way. Marie followed her guide's bare feet, watching them sink into the sand and kick it backward at each step.

Pierre stooped, plucked a stem with bright green leaves, and turned around. "Try this," he said. "It makes good soup. People keep it all winter long. See, the leaf with three points. Taste." She tasted, and the flavor of very ripe fruit flooded her mouth.

Near the rocks the sandstrip died out, and they entered the forest along a grass-grown path. Thrushes fluttered aloft in alarm, and a jumping mouse hopped swiftly away.

On either side thick pine trunks thrust up from impenetrable banks of fern. At head level were the lowest boughs with thousands of reddish needles, thick, dry bristles that were dying for want of light. Higher up, the dark green of the living branches splintered the blue of the sky.

They crossed a clearing overgrown with sumac. Then a stand of maples, with one or two big silver birches whose bark was peeling from the trunks like the open pages of a book.

On the other side of the forest you could hear the sea. Then they were at Pierre's cabin. Sitting in front of it was the policeman.

Pierre hesitated and stopped.

It was Marie who stepped forward, her "Good afternoon" sounding new, forced, withdrawn. The policeman rose heavily.

"What are you doing here?" he said.

"What do you mean, what am I doing!" said Marie. "I've come to buy herring. And sardine, if there are any."

"Uh-huh!"

"Is it against the law?"

"Nope. It's mighty odd, though. Do you come here often?"

"Sometimes."

"How many times?"

"I don't know."

The policemen looked at them both and frowned.

"And what have you got to say for yourself, Le Rouge?" he said.

"Le Rouge," Marie shrugged angrily. "Le Rouge has nothing to say. He's a mute. Maybe he's crazy. Everyone says he is."

"Uh-huh."

"In fact, that's why I come over here. If you want herring, you have to be right here. Otherwise he might bring you anything. So."

"Your parents send you? Be mighty surprised if they did."

"I don't need my parents, as you call them, to go out and buy fish."

"Bit fresh, aren't you? Let's have some manners. Otherwise your dad will warm your backside for you."

"It wouldn't be the first time," said Marie.

"What's in the bag?" said the policeman.

"No bomb; no matches; no teddy bear. Books. Want to see? Books. So." She shrugged and turned to Pierre:

"Well, Mister, can you sell me some herring? Or sardine?"

"Hold it, kid: don't mess with me! You're coming with me, and don't give me any trouble. I'm taking you home . . . and keep your mouth shut! By force if I have to. This is the second time I've seen you waiting outside your house. Waiting for him. I saw you . . . and I want to know where you get to and what you're playing at. Uh-huh!" He looked her up and down, then went on. "Your parents are going to hear about this. And you, Le Rouge, if I see you with her one more time, just one more time, I'm locking you up. Understand? In prison. In-pri-son. Got it?" He shook his finger at Pierre. "And what are all those newspapers doing on your wall? Looks mighty fishy to me. We put up with you around here as long as you stayed put and behaved yourself. But if you bother us, you're going inside. Got it?"

The policeman then turned to Marie. "All right, girl, move! In front. The car's over there. Get going."

Marie was already walking in the direction of the car. She turned toward Pierre: "Goodbye, Mister."

"Quiet, and move!" said the policeman.

Why was he taking her away? Pierre couldn't understand it. He stood still and watched them move off through the trees. Marie turned round twice and smiled both times. They disappeared at the end of the path, and there was the sound of a car starting up and leaving.

Who's going to teach me the missing letters? Pierre thought.

He was confused, bewildered; his mind was racing, going through what had just happened, looking for an explanation, searching for an answer, trying to find a reason: He said he saw us, twice. I wasn't watching, because I was with Marie. It's my fault, I didn't watch. He said: "If you bother us." That's what he said. He doesn't like me to be with Marie; it bothers him. Why? He's afraid I'll hurt her. Maybe that I'll kill her. He doesn't know she's teaching me to read and write.

That's it. He would tell him—that she was teaching him to read and write. Because he never went to school. "And how are you doing?" the policeman would say. And he'd reply that he was doing quite well, but it takes time. It's not hard, no, but it takes time. So we have to go fast, and so we see each other every day. So! There are lots of letters still. . . .

Pierre shook himself from his thoughts. He realized he hadn't told the policeman anything. Worry gave way to fear, fear that the policeman was going to take her home to the white house, to her parents. Perhaps they'd yell. Perhaps he'd beat her. If she cried, it would be his fault because he had said nothing to the policeman.

"I've come to buy herring, and sardine. . . ." That's what Marie had said. Why? She had called him Mister. If only Marie were here, if she were here to explain, he'd understand. She hadn't wanted the policeman to know. Why? And he had just listened without doing anything.

Pierre sat down in front of the cabin, his brow furrowed with lines of pain. Then he got up and went inside. The policeman's feet had left earth and twigs on the wooden floor. Pierre looked at the letters stuck on his wall.

He went out.

Once again Pierre looked out at the sea, at the gulf glowing with heat all the way to the Iles.

"Marie. Marie," he whispered. "When you looked at the sea you asked, *'What's it like on the other shore?'*"

"It's the land of my mother Nod."

"And beyond that?"

"The land that has no end."

"I know. All the way to the North Pole. And it's the same again beyond. I know: the Land of Cain."

"There's nothing there."

"There are animals that kill each other."

"There are enormous forests."

"Animals on the earth and under the earth as well."

"You can walk through the forest all winter and by spring it still hasn't ended."

"Animals in the sky and on the water."

"You can walk all summer through the swampland and the prairies, and by the end of the summer the prairies haven't ended."

"There are a hundred thousand lakes, but no one knows them."

"Then come ice and snow. You can walk all winter. You reach another sea. You can cross that too, they say, and on the other shore is another land."

"There are flowers too, hidden flowers. More beautiful than the flowers here: the most beautiful flowers in the world. But no one has ever seen them."

"You can walk another full season and reach other seas and other lands, and after that I don't know. It never ends."

"You and I could go there."

"No. We would die."

"We would live. With the animals and flowers, with the lakes and streams. We would be alone, we could do as we liked."

"We would get lost."

"We wouldn't be going anywhere, so we couldn't get lost!"

"Marie. Marie," he whispered. He knew now that he had to go there, to the clearing. If he went along the shore, no one would see him. And when he reached the foot of the Cape, he'd follow the rocks and beach along the tide line. To below the white house. Then he'd climb up to the rocks, quietly, without making a sound, and he'd sit and wait for her. Maybe she'd come. If she wasn't there by dark, he'd come back down and go back again tomorrow.

The sun was sinking behind the big white house. Trees and sky, rocks and grass were bathed in fiery ochre. Everything glowed like liquid gold. Pierre slipped between the two rocks in the clearing, and there was Marie. She threw her arms around him.

They laughed as they held each other. Then she drew back to see Pierre's face more clearly.

"I knew you'd come right away," she said. "I was waiting for you. We'll have to find a safer spot, you know."

Pierre thought hard. And Marie added:

"They're drunk. Hah! Good for them! So he said he'd talk to them tomorrow. The oaf! What business is it of his? You should've seen his face. What a laugh!"

"There's the hole, maybe," Pierre said.

"What hole?"

"The spring... it dug out a hole behind the flat rock. It's almost on the edge of the gulf. You can't see the hole, it's between two big boulders. One winter a lynx lived in it, because of the catnip that grew around there all summer. Lynx love the smell. It was the only one I've ever seen around here. Usually they stay on the other side of the gulf, in the land that has no end, up in the north. We could go to the hole every day, and nobody'd know. If we're careful."

"And where is the flat rock? I'll go there tomorrow."

"Tomorrow when the tide will be going out. You can go along by the rocks where the Cape begins. I'll be waiting there, and I'll show you the way to the hole."

"Is it underground?"

"No. And it's big. You can sit down. It's cool in summer."

"I'll tell them I wanted herring. They couldn't care less, anyway. The oaf! He's wasting his time."

"But if you tell them you're teaching me to read?"

"Are you crazy? You don't know them. They'd watch me night and day."

"Why?"

"That's how it is, that's all."

Pierre sensed that this was true. He sensed that Marie was right. They mustn't say anything, they mustn't be seen. Maybe Marie was crying that day because they had stopped her doing something, something she liked doing. Like seeing him, and sitting near him, and listening to him talk. That's when her eyes would get big and shiny. They would wander away, over to the land of his mother Nod, across the gulf in winter, into the forests. Her lips would be open and she would sit still, and that's when he knew she was happy. And when she was telling him things, too. She liked to tell him things, and explain. Even when she was teaching him all the letters she would look as happy as he was.

But when she was crying she hadn't met him. That day. What was it then?

"Now," said Marie. "I have to go. I'm going to eat before they wake up. See you tomorrow then? I'll be at the bottom of the Cape, and we'll go to the spring."

"Show me one more letter," said Pierre. "Just one."

"Today we were supposed to do *M.* Wait. Give me your knife." Slowly, as Pierre watched, she scraped at the blue rock, then stepped back to judge her work. She had drawn two clumsy letters.

"There you are. The capital and the small one. That's enough. You can easily remember, it's the only one with three legs. See? One, two, three. Make the sound: *me, me, me* . . ."

Lips closed, Pierre repeated the sound. She went on: "With *a,* it makes *ma! Ma, ma* . . . and you know how it goes with the other letters. So. I have to go. I really must. That oaf is probably still somewhere around. I don't trust him. And if they're awake, I want to be there. See you at the flat rock tomorrow."

She ran away. Pierre stared at the carving on the rock. Then he went down the slope and took the track along the bay shore. At each step he repeated the new letter. With a sudden thought in between: Marie isn't in prison. Ma, me, mi, my, mo, mu . . .

Three legs.

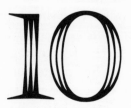

Next day they went together to the source of the spring.

Just as Pierre had said, it was a big cavity, hollowed out beneath huge, precariously balanced boulders that almost came together overhead. But one side of the cave let in the light, and that was how you got inside.

On the floor were sand, weeds, ferns, wormwood, and even a few buttercups. Water seeped halfheartedly from one stony corner a little away from the light. You couldn't tell exactly where it came from. First there was damp soil and saturated moss, then a sluggish trickle, then iridescent puddles. Finally a thin, feeble stream appeared, wound between two granite boulders, went underground, and came up again outside the cave, where it flowed downhill toward the gulf.

Dead leaves and branches had piled up in sheltered corners where the wind never reached. As Pierre began to clear them out, Marie marveled at their new meeting place. "This is just what we needed," she said. "No one will ever find us here. You're a genius, Pierre! Let me help you." She picked up a branch and swept the leaves aside.

"And now," she said, once they were settled, "here's my present: the dictionary. Of course I had it yesterday, but I couldn't show it to you because of that oaf."

"The policeman comes to see me sometimes," said Pierre. "I'm glad when he shows up. But yesterday . . . We talk a bit, he asks me if it's the right time to hunt or go fishing. He buys furs and game from me, too. Once, one winter, he even brought me some potatoes. I sold him a beaver. . . ."

"Hah! I knew there was a catch!" said Marie. "Did you notice when we got to the cabin? He was all steamed up. Who does he think he is? If I'd been with one of our neighbors from the Cape, or with those two dirty little idiots from next door, he wouldn't have said a thing. But I was with you, so he was boiling mad. You understand?"

"No, why?"

"Whenever you want to do things you like they stop you. So. You don't understand, do you? It doesn't matter, you'll understand some day. . . . And how much did you sell the beaver for? Just to see?"

"One dollar."

"I don't believe it!" said Marie. "When are you going to stop letting yourself get robbed like that? No, listen, Pierre, you're just being stupid! I'm really mad at you. The other day you told me the campers at the end of the bay gave you a dollar for all your sardines. Well, okay! But a beaver's worth more than sardines, isn't it? It's worth a fortune! So!" She looked at him reprovingly.

"I know you don't care," she went on. "That's your privilege. But it isn't *their* privilege! They're crooks. Don't you understand?"

"No."

"Oh, listen!"

"But I like to meet people," said Pierre. "Even the policeman. They scare me a little, but not when I know them or when they come to my place. I like it, and I talk to them. So I don't care about the beaver. I could catch lots more."

Pierre picked up the dictionary and leafed through a few pages.

"It's a beautiful dictionary," he said. "Look, it's the way you said, there are pictures and photos. And pages, all these pages! It's the biggest book I've ever seen."

"Yet for a dictionary it's quite a small one, you know. They use it for crossword puzzles. They need to look up spellings all the time. What a scene there'll be when they find it missing! He'll say she threw it away. She'll say she didn't. Then there'll be shouting and he'll go through the whole house, my room too, maybe I should sneak out. . . . 'She did it, I bet she did it!' I can hear him now." Marie smiled at Pierre, who was engrossed, flipping back and forth through the dictionary. Suddenly he looked up.

"Now I'll give you my present," he said.

He emptied his bag. Books, the notebook, and pencils all piled up on the grass beside the dictionary. Pierre handed Marie a small white cone. She examined it from all angles in silence, then turned it round and round in her fingers. She felt the softness of the ivory, as smooth as glass and warming slowly in her hands. The tooth was at once hard and as soft as a petal. She held it to her lips, giving herself an enormous canine fang, and looked at Pierre. They both laughed. Then she gave the tooth a kiss.

"It's beautiful," she said a little later, laying it against her breast. "Beautiful. If it had a hole, I could put it on a chain or a leather thong. It would make a fabulous pendant. It will be you, Pierre. I'll be carrying you around my neck. For ever. Whenever I touch the tooth I'll think of you. And I'll think of that poor orca who ate so much, the beast! He stuffed himself with seal and then they stole the lot! Good for them! And I'll have his last tooth. It'll be you, Pierre."

"But you know," said Pierre, "seals are just like beaver. There are lots of them. More than beaver, many more! So many you can't begin to imagine. Once I saw a whole herd. There were as many of them as all the ice floes in the gulf. And I saw a big herd of bearded seal once. The only time I've ever seen them in these parts."

"So? . . . Well?"

"That was last winter. They have the best leather. I made moccasins."

"How did you kill it?"

"With my rifle."

"That must've hurt."

"It couldn't have. Just one shot. The others didn't even move."

"It's nice here," said Marie. "It's a fabulous day. They can look all they want. We'll come here every day."

"And we'll study all the letters that are left?"

"Do you want to go on now?"

"Yes."

"It's a beautiful tooth. But I'll have to keep it under my dresses so that no one will see it. Pick up your notebook. We'll do a dictation with the letter I showed you yesterday. I hope you remember it."

When Pierre had finished writing, Marie showed him N.

"I'd better warn you," she said. "It's going to be tricky now, because N is so much like M. Listen carefully to the difference: 'Ma, Na."

"Ma. Na."

"Oh, yes! Good, you can say it now. That's very good, you catch on so fast. I remember when I was learning to read I mixed them up for a long time. The nuns said, 'We're sorry, but you'll have to be punished.' I didn't care, I liked writing in my notebook, and the punishment was to write out pages of M's and N's instead of playing in the yard. I didn't like playing. Now I play all the time. When I read a book I play all the characters. I even make them up."

"What nuns?"

"In the orphanage," she said, then, seeing his puzzled look, she added, "Don't you know what that is?"

"Yes, but I've never seen one."

"It was before they came to get me. I was six or seven."

"Ma . . . it sounds as if you're going to say 'Marie.'"

"Yes."

"So you can't confuse it with *Na*."

"Oh, no? You make me laugh. Just you wait! But try and remember which one has only two legs."

"Not you. You have three legs," said Pierre. "Why were you in the orphanage?"

"Look, here are the other two *n*'s. This one's for writing, and this one's for reading. See. Write them down."

Pierre complied obediently.

"The orphanage was for kids," Marie continued. "There were lots of them, and people came to adopt them. There was one nun who liked me a lot. She took care of me, she said I was sick. I forget her name. She used to say, 'The others find parents before you do because you're sick.' . . . Have you finished? Look at the book. . . . See, if you put the two syllables together you get *Ma-Ma*. Just like your mother."

"Mama. Like my mother Nod."

"Yes. We could write her name, too. Give me the notebook," said Marie. "I assume it's written *N-o-d. Nod*. With the big *N*, the capital. You always put a capital in front of people's names, remember? It's a strange name."

"Her real Indian name is Seal's Blood."

"I know. Your father was a funny person. I'd have liked to meet him. I'd have had a few things to say to him!"

Pierre could remember his father far better than before. Ever since Marie has been asking questions and he'd been trying to answer.

"I remember how he didn't say anything for days," Pierre told Marie. "He'd read the newspapers, then put them back in the envelope. Then he wouldn't speak. 'He is thinking of his ancestors,' my mother Nod would say. 'Leave him alone. If you follow him, he'll hit you with his whip, and so will I.' But one time when my father left I went out, too, and followed him from a distance. He didn't look at anything, not even the jackrabbit run or the snares. Suddenly he stopped. I was afraid he had heard me. I stopped breathing. Then he started again. I waited till he was far away. I was at the foot of a maple. I was bored. I listened as the crows started cawing again. Then I went back to the cabin. He didn't come back till it was evening, or maybe night. My mother gave him soup or a fish or something. He ate it without speaking. Then we went to bed. Sometimes he went back into the woods at night, and the dog growled to go with him. I heard. That went on for several days, and then he said, 'Come on,' and I could go with him again. . . . He used to say, 'Never trust anyone.'"

"Why?"

"I don't know."

"It's terrible, nobody took any care of you."

"What about you? Were you really sick at the orphanage?"

"No! But if I'd known, I'd have pretended to be. That way, no parents! I was better off at the orphanage than with them."

"They've taken care of you."

"Them. So what?"

"I don't know."

Marie looked at him. Her face was very pale and smooth, without the slightest wrinkle, without even a freckle, and under her silky eyebrows her eyes were bright. "It's warm here," she said. "It's nice." And a little later: "The nicest place I was ever in was the orphanage. And here with you."

Summer burned on endlessly. It was the hottest year of all. None of the summer people could remember it being like this on the Cape. And worst of all was the August humidity, which had lasted longer than usual. "We come here to get away from the humidity down south. This year we needn't have bothered," they grumbled one evening. Marie said nothing; she listened; she shrugged her shoulders. Hidden away with Pierre every day, she didn't care about the humidity. She stood in the hazy twilight and watched the sun drown like an orange in the mists of the bay. Next day she told Pierre what she had seen the night before: "I saw dolphin yesterday. There were at least a dozen. Fantastic."

"Sunset—that means they were hungry. In the morning it would be to scratch."

"To what?"

"That's what people say: they come to the surface to kill the lice on their skins. It makes them feel better. But the weather will change soon," said Pierre.

And for two long weeks drought set in. The lilacs shriveled where they stood; the earth panted; smoke blew in from vast distances, smelling of burned pine and carrying frenzied swarms of flies. The only memory of coolness in the land came from the occasional whiff of mildew that arose from dead trees, half-fallen, splintered, and slimy with rot, in the depths of the high forest. The sea was a burnished mirror, reflecting the naked, heavy sky deep into the night. Then the moonlight blended with the aurora to streak the heavens with whey from horizon to horizon. From his bed Pierre could hear every rustle, every sound. The forest was alive with animals out to seek the cool air. In the morning there was dew, but only for minutes. It evaporated almost at once.

During that time Marie wore a long, thin, beltless dress, like a cape with the sleeves cut off; it rippled at her slightest movement. When she sat down she gathered the material round her on the ground. She looked like a big, fading, salmon-pink flower that was dropped over the grass, head first and crestfallen.

Every day she waited impatiently for noon, gazing beyond the dark wood that crowned the Cape, craning her neck to see the distant outline of mountains framed between branches to the south. She followed the progress of the day on their wooded flanks: when the tops of the maple and pine began to gleam, then gradually turn pale, it would mean that noon was near and the sun would start to drop toward the bay. Then everything would grow bright and warm and sleepy amid the honey-sweet perfume of bees. And Pierre would set out from his woods to come and meet her.

He wanted to learn to read. And she waited for him. "I'm always in a hurry to get away," she would say to him. Or, "They're still on their *apéritif,* they'll never be finished. I eat a sandwich or something—the quicker the better—then, wham! I find an excuse to get out. I go to pick strawberries (that's what I tell them) or to take a swim. I get the books and I sneak out. I go by roundabout ways so no one will know where I am, and then I'm in our hiding place waiting for you. . . ."

Often she read, her back to a rock, the heavy odor of earth and lichen rising all round her. "This is the best place of all for reading. When I read a poem here it's as if music were floating up to me from the gulf. Just now I was reading a story about pirates and a treasure island. I'm not kidding, you scared me when you showed up. Wow! You had a wooden leg and a patch over one eye. . . . I'd like to have a parrot. . . ."

Pierre was impatient from the moment he got up. He neglected jobs he had always taken care of: cutting and piling wood (his woodpile was shrinking); or working on his vegetable garden, which was beginning to look like a wilderness. He made just one trip a day to the stream for water. He went down to the beach to empty his dam. The sky had the first faint metallic blue of dawn. Far away, porpoise rose and fell rhythmically off the Iles. Pierre was in a hurry. When summer was over Marie would be gone. He'd be alone, and then he'd get wood and all the rest. This winter. Not now. She'll be waiting for him at noon.

He rarely went to see the campers on the beach at the end of the bay. They always wanted sardine or herring, and they weren't too plentiful this year. And going to see them and talk to them took up too much time. He preferred to write or read in his cabin or by the door. He read out loud all the letters and sounds Marie had taught him. He was always thinking of her.

Sometimes he sat by the radio, turned it on, and listened. After a while, he turned it off, bored. He looked at the sky. It would soon be noon, and Marie would be sitting against a rock in the hole under the spring.

When he got there he saw her smiling. She looked up and said: "This is stupid; it's about a girl called Alice. But it makes me laugh so much! It's full of funny stuff. . . . Good afternoon, Pierre."

Then, as he sat down next to her, she asked, "What do you dream of when you sleep?"

"Me? I don't know."

"I always dream. Every night. Sometimes I remember a long time afterward. But never the way it is in here." She showed him the illustrations. Pierre thought they were funny.

"Do you know how many different books there are?" she said. "Just to see? More than there are people in the whole world! People die all the time. They're a bore. Books never die. So!"

"What about you and me? Will we die, too?"

"I guess."

"Even if we take good care?"

"You smiled! You're laughing at me, aren't you?"

"I think about it a lot," said Pierre.

"I don't, it's stupid."

"What will we do . . . after?"

"You're funny! We're sure to meet loads of interesting people. I'd like to talk to Ulysses and Captain Nemo. When I was young I used to tell people what I'd do when I was dead. They laughed at me: 'Still dreaming about impossible things, eh?' 'Why impossible?' I'd reply. 'Oh, for heaven's sake, come off that cloud! You and your books, you're too much!' But my books have interesting people in them, nice people, clever people. Just like you!"

"Did they write books?"

"Who?"

"Those people you'd like to meet?"

"What? Oh, them. No, no, they're *in* books. People who write books—I don't care whether I meet them or not."

Then Marie began to sing. Pierre sat quite still, making himself as small and silent as he could. Whenever she sang he would try to understand the words, but they would get all mixed up and he would just follow the music. Marie would often sing the same song over and over again; then she would stop. Pierre would sit still. A little later she would start again. He could hardly hear the words. But it was nice. After she'd finished, he wouldn't dare say anything for a long time. Perhaps, he thought, she was going to start again.

It was always Marie who broke the silence:

"It's hot, isn't it? I'd like to go swimming soon. You

never swim, do you? That's weird. You just wash. I get cold right away in the sea. . . . I never stay in long, you know."

Or else: "Tell me about your father. Why did he stay there in that cabin with your mother and you?"

"I don't know. Maybe he would've told me if he hadn't disappeared."

"It's a pity."

"But I remember him saying, 'If you live with people, you end up being like them.'"

"That's good!"

"You think so? I didn't understand it too well, just a little. I understood that he didn't trust anyone, the way he told me."

"Well, that time your father was right. You know, maybe I like him a little after all; sometimes he sounds a bit like me. 'She doesn't like anybody,' they say. 'She's proud, who does she think she is?' But it isn't true. Every time I meet a person they tell me stupid things and annoy me and I finish up sticking my tongue out at them. So! . . . Yes, it's a pity. I'll think of him some time, when I'm out looking at the mud flats in the evening. Just to see . . . you know . . ."

"And my father said, 'Never lose your temper.'"

"But he beat you!"

"No."

"You told me . . . with his whip. I remember."

"He hadn't lost his temper."

One day, after they had been studying, she suggested a picnic. "I'll fix it," she said. "I already left for the whole day once before. They don't care. I'll bring everything. We'll go and pick berries—you know, the big ones, blueberries. There are lots of

121

them. In the old peat bogs behind the wood. It's a long way, I went there last year, but it's nice, there won't be anybody there. Let's meet there tomorrow, okay? At ten. . . . You haven't even got a watch, dummy!" she laughed.

Pierre laughed too, but the next morning he was there on time.

You had to climb up through a wood that was drowsy with heat. It was at the end of the bay, and you could hear the campers' voices down on the beach. The trees came to an end at the top, and they walked down a recently deforested slope, startling jays as they went.

The old swamps at the bottom of the peat bogs were choked with brambles, wildflowers, and huckleberry heavy with fruit.

They went from bush to bush, picking the small blue-velvet berries. Often there were so many bunches on the same bush that Marie would settle comfortably beside it and stay a long time, determined to strip the whole bush. But she never finished: a neighboring bush, equally laden with berries, would soon tempt her to move.

A jackrabbit suddenly broke from cover. They stood and watched its frantic leaps, then it was gone. The heat rose around them, fiercer than ever on this desolate stretch of ground that seemed to throw back the sun's warmth. Little whorls of hot air, transparent yet visible, deformed the foliage as they spiraled upward and disappeared in the blue of the sky. A flock of blackbird landed all around them on the berry-laden brambles. The air smelled of rancid honey and dried peat. As the sun gradually sank toward the larches at the end of the clearing, thousands of flowers of every variety shone with heightened color in the mild light of midafternoon. They were in an enormous garden, with rows of daisies, long alleyways of blue thistle, tall violet clover, buttercups, and dandelion. On the sumacs at the end of the clearing fire-red clusters of berries crackled against the velvet-green backdrop of the trees. Near them, tall foxgloves held spears of pink blossoms aloft, each one a cone of buzzing wasps.

Marie stretched out, arms spread wide, crucified in the grass, drunk on scent and bright sun. "I'm tired," she said. "I can't go on. Isn't this heavenly? I could stay here till night if you were with me."

She closed her eyes. Pierre sat beside her. She breathed evenly, then twisted her body a little, hollowing out a place for herself in the grass. Pierre looked at the still form beside him. He wondered if she cried often. But maybe that day was different from others, he thought. It must have been different: Marie wasn't like the children he'd seen who cry for nothing and whose parents slap them, or who throw stones and laugh at him. When Marie laughed, she was beautiful, and then he would laugh, too, right away. He wondered if it might have been for something very important, important enough to make her cry. He wanted to ask her why she had been crying that day.

"I'm not asleep," she said. "Don't you want to say anything? . . . Tell me what you're thinking, just to see."

"I'm thinking that you're happy."

"Oh, yes."

She opened her eyes, blinked slightly in the dazzling light, and turned her face to him:

"This year is my best vacation ever. It was never as good as this year. And it's because of you. It's because I met you. It's so good just to be with you! Nobody's watching us or talking to us. And I'm not scared. I'm not scared of anything. I'd like to stay this way for ever." She plucked a blade of grass and nibbled at it.

"I'll go to your house," she went on. "It must be nice there, as nice as here, maybe even nicer, because it's your house. The policeman won't always be there. He came once and said his piece and now he's happy. He won't come back. I'm certain. But I don't know if I could go there in winter. How do you keep it warm? A cooking range or a stove isn't much. I don't know if I could. . . . He said he'd lock you up, the oaf."

"This is a fine place," said Pierre. "Nobody comes here. I've seen hunters come across the prairie there in autumn, looking for partridge. But not now. The hole under the spring is good, too."

"Yes," said Marie. She sat up.

She took sandwiches from her straw bag and laid them out on the grass. There were paper napkins, two bottles of a colorless drink, and straws. Marie unwrapped the glittering paper and gave him a sandwich. She watched as he chewed a mouthful.

"Good?"

"Yes," said Pierre.

"I made them this morning. They don't bother me in the morning, they're asleep. I make fantastic meals! Whatever I feel like. Eggs with sugar is good."

"Oh, yes?"

"Maple sugar. Or syrup. I couldn't bring any, we'd

need matches and a stove. But I'll make you some. With ham, too, it's great. I put all the nicest things I could find in these. Do you like them?"

Pierre's mouth was full; he was deliriously happy. He could taste each mouthful. It was food Marie had made, it was full of sweet, tender tastes, tastes he'd never had before.

"Have a drink," said Marie. "After, there's bananas and oranges. And we can eat as many blueberries as we like." She was just nibbling. She handed Pierre another sandwich.

"Eat up, I'm not very hungry," she said. "It's too hot. I like to watch you eat. You should eat fruit, and salad, and vegetables. That's what they say. Because of the vitamins: I won't explain that to you because it's too complicated."

"I do eat them," said Pierre. "I have a garden. In winter as well. I have my potatoes."

"I don't like potatoes. They have no taste. Ugghh! Even sweet ones. Believe me, I'll be thinking of you this winter. I'll be worried."

"Well, I'll be happy knowing that you're thinking of me, and if you want, I'll eat everything you say."

"I'd rather be here. I don't trust you. Eat some more."

But he wasn't hungry anymore. Marie's sharp eyes were watching him, and he forced himself to eat a banana. It had no taste. Marie said, "Put all the rest in your bag. That's right. For tonight or tomorrow. I'm tired of picking berries. Do you want to work?"

"Yes."

"At first," said Marie, "you didn't give a hoot about learning to read. You hadn't even thought about it. I was the one who said you were crazy, and I was right. There's nothing better than books. So! I'll never change my mind. But now, wow! are you in a hurry! Worse than me.... In fact, I wonder.... That isn't the only reason you come to see me, is it? Come on now, let's have the truth!"

Astounded, Pierre stared at Marie. "No," he said. "I come to see you, too, to talk to you, because I like the things you tell me."

"Do you really think so?"

"I don't know.... Yes."

"Ah," said Marie, and burst out laughing. Pierre smiled.

They started to work.

Much later, when they were both tired of reading, writing, and studying, they dozed. Pierre leaned against the burnt stump of a pine, and Marie lay on the ground, her cheek resting on the softness of dead moss.

"What's nice," she said, "is that you're not like somebody you meet every day. You're different. You could easily go into a book and make yourself right at home and stay there until the last page.... I bet I'd love that! See, it's just like that: just like closing a book I've been reading. To take a rest until tomorrow. Tomorrow I'll meet you; I'll feel good again with you, the way I feel now, next to you. I'm going to teach you more letters and words, and you'll learn them at top speed. Because you're very intelligent. And all the things you tell me are going to go round and round my head all evening. And all night. Till tomorrow."

"Before," said Pierre, "I liked to talk to people. I asked things. They asked me, too. I made them laugh.

I knew they were making fun of me. . . . I wasn't sure why. But I didn't care. I was happy. But when I'm with you I listen. You never make fun of me. I understand everything you say. Now I like listening better."

He closed his eyes. The smell of mint wafted to him from a nearby bush.

"But soon you'll leave. When summer's over. And I'll be alone."

"When you reach a certain age," said Marie, "you can go off on your own and no one can stop you. They call you a major. Then they can't bother you, no one can. That's lucky, eh? We'll have to wait until then, until I get to be of age, otherwise they only bring you back again. . . . I'll wait."

Marie lowered her eyes. She examined her bare arm under the short sleeve of her blouse. A tiny, blue-speckled fly had settled on it. Marie nodded sharply to attract Pierre's attention, then sat perfectly still. In a low voice she said:

"Flies are interesting. Don't you think so? Did you ever hear anyone say they liked flies? No one. They see a fly and yukkh! they squash it. They'll kill them like flies." She laughed.

"Hello, fly," she breathed, keeping so still that the insect did not move. Then it began to walk across Marie's arm; she shook it off, gurgling with laughter. The fly darted into the air. "You tickled me, you dummy," she said. "He could've stayed there if he'd kept still. But he's just a poor dumb fly, and that's why I love him. . . . Things like that—flies, toads, snakes—people hate them. They must feel sad all the time. It's terrible. So I hate people who hate them. So! They can all die!"

The stillness of the leaves around them was complete: they were cast in metal. In the distance, great sweeps of forest drowned in light resembled blurred, ashen mountain ranges, their contours uncertain, their fluid forms almost transparent in the treacly heat. Crumpled on the ground, enormous rhubarb fronds turned brown. They gave off a faint smell of dung.

Pierre said: "I know snakes pretty well. I've never killed one, did you know?"

"Oh, you . . . of course not!" said Marie.

They made their way back slowly. Just before she left him, near the Cape, Marie gave nearly all her blueberries to Pierre: "Eat them, they're good for you, believe me. I'll just take a few back. For them. I'm full." He watched her walk toward the gravel road, a dark silhouette amid the swirling flowered currents of the prairie. It was the purple hour, the hour of the departed sun.

In the next few days new signs appeared in the bay.

The water was colder, even at high tide. Nobody swam anymore. Long strands of dead algae floated in the troughs of waves, and gulls bobbed meekly up and down as if befuddled by the cold. In the hollows of rocks by the shore, grass that had been dried by salt was no longer able to grow green again. It was still hot during the day, but by evening you were shivering, and the houses on the Cape switched their lights on early.

Little by little the campers were thinning out. Every morning another tent came down, another trailer pulled away. Pierre cut firewood from dawn till noon, then went to meet Marie at the spring. One morning he saw the last cormorant on the gulf. He was sure it was the last. The greenish, almost-black bird was drying itself on a rock, its wings spread open to the breeze. Its head lay back on its snakelike neck, its hooked beak pointing skyward. At last it rose, floundering in its feathers, and took off sluggishly over the waves. Suddenly it seemed to lose weight, and beat steadily eastward out to sea. Pierre was sure it was the last cormorant on the gulf.

Gradually the colors were coming back to life. As if the summer heat had dulled the splendor of the bay under its uniform veil of light, the exact tone of things reappeared as soon as the sun had lost its harshness: the sea was streaked green and brown by its currents; the mud flats bristled with rocks on which the smallest red lichen glowed; pink sandy beaches were dotted with the flittering mauve of baby mussels; and riverbanks were turbulent with different shades of greenery, slashed by the black plumes of pines and scarred by bright silver birch.

And Marie, a sweater thrown across her shoulders, dictated:

"*A rose,* comma, *two roses,* period. Don't forget the capital now. *The cherry,* comma, *two cherries,* period. *One cabbage,* comma, *two cabbages,* period. (That's right, two *b*'s.) *The strawberries are ripe,* period. Do you understand plurals now? Well, we've finished them."

She was on the next to last page of their reader. She watched Pierre finish writing, then checked the dictation.

There were no mistakes. Pierre's writing had greatly improved. Marie took the notebook, turned back to the beginning, and smiled as she looked at his first letters, huge and malformed compared with those of the last few days.

She turned to the last page of the reader and said, "They've written out the alphabet at the end so that you can revise the whole thing. Here, see? Read it."

Pierre read all the letters. Now they had really finished the book. Marie put it down and looked at Pierre.

"There: you know all the letters, every letter in existence!" she said. "And you know how to put them together to make every sound in existence. Do you realize how learned you are?"

Lost in wonder, Pierre strained to grasp the idea that he could now read and write. These last few days he had known that the time was near, he had sensed that the things he had learned were coming together—punctuation, capitals, the sounds made by letters in groups, plurals. He had sensed that they all fitted together, balancing and completing each other like the trees and the grass, the earth, the sand, and the rocks, the sea, the birds, and the sky; that they all made up a whole. Now he forced his mind to focus on that whole: it was a new joy, a new lightness, a violent urge to leap, to jump, to yell. But Marie's presence, the whiteness of her face, his own laughter that was infecting her and heightening his own pleasure—all these combined to disperse his mood. He felt extremely complicated.

Suddenly warmth flooded him. He could read and write! He got up and shuffled a few dance steps. Marie laughed, then she, too, got up and took Pierre's hands. Singing out a rhythm, she pulled him into a sort of twosome reel, and they whirled round and round in the narrow confines of their hiding place. Soon they were laughing madly, drunk on their closeness and complicity. Gradually they tired, stumbling over stones and clumps of grass, clutching at each other for support. Then Marie threw herself to the ground: "I can't go on! Whew! Oh, I'm so happy, I'm so happy!" Pierre leaned against a rock, out of breath, and watching her.

After a while she said, "Come over here. Sit down. There, yes. Now, take the pencil and sign your name. Write. Write the two sounds: PI-ERRE. . . . There, that's good. Pierre. See? Anyone in the whole world can read that: Pierre. Everyone in the world knows your name just by reading it. They know that it's you you're talking about. You don't need to say it, it's written. Pierre. It's you."

He looked at the page. It was him. It said his name: Pierre. A small sob rose in his throat. Marie thought that perhaps he was still out of breath. No, she could see it was something else. She took Pierre's hand, raised it to her lips, and kissed it. "There," she said. "That's your reward.

"Obviously," she went on, "if you knew your other name, I mean your father's name, you would add that, too. Then it would really be you. You and no one else. . . ."

"Are you going to leave now?" said Pierre.

"No, not yet! What an idea! I've already told you, we leave in the middle of September. Don't think about it. We still have things to learn, you haven't finished yet. I know, we'll start another book right away. You have to keep practicing. . . . Maybe your father's name is in those newspaper articles, in that envelope you told me about? No? Why did you never bring it to me?"

"I don't know. He used to say, 'My name? It's just as stupid as Seal's Blood!'"

"That doesn't matter. If you want to know it, all you have to do now is read it yourself. So."

"The middle of September is soon."

"Oh, be quiet," said Marie. "I know."

"I looked at the book last night. And I saw it was nearly finished."

"So you knew last night that we'd finish it today?"

"And I saw the gannet fly away, too."

"Are they the ones from the north?"

"Yes," said Pierre. "They fly south every fall. Just like you. I didn't know what to do. I was sad. I thought for a long time before I went to sleep."

He could have opened his father's envelope that night. He had thought he would be able to read the newspaper articles, even if he had to skip words. But he didn't. He had waited. He had lain there, thinking of the geese and of Marie. He had decided he would open the envelope when Marie had gone. Just to see, as she used to say.

"And this morning," said Pierre, "there wasn't a single petrel left in the small cliff behind my cabin. Petrel always leave at night, you know, and no one sees them go. In the morning they've gone. The gulls and the ferrets go and inspect their rookeries, but it's too late, they're empty. They've gone."

"Well, they go to a warm place. That's not so dumb! But you stay here, I don't know how you manage. I'm going to be worried."

"Not all of them," said Pierre. "Some go north, to the land of my mother Nod."

"Oh."

"But they come back. They all come back in spring."

"So? So I'll come back, too! I've told you, all you have to do is wait. And take good care of yourself. And work hard. To learn to read, as hard as you can. To read as well as me. So."

"Yes," Pierre said softly.

He was crouched beside Marie. He felt the coolness in the air, snaking in through the ferns and nipping at his ankles, hands, and neck. There were some aspen leaves, already turned yellow, on the floor. A gull squawked continuously somewhere down on the rocks.

"But perhaps next year they won't want to come back to the bay," he said.

"The birds?"

"Your parents."

"Everyone leaves town in summer. So will they: you can count on it!"

"I'll wait for spring," said Pierre. "I'll come here every day to see if you're back. But perhaps next year you'll forget to come?"

"What's the matter with you? Next year I'll be waiting for spring, too. And the very first day I arrive, pow! I'll be here. I'll come to the cabin right away to let you know. And I'll bring you a whole bunch of things. I'll save them for you all winter. A whole bunch of things."

Marie was huddled under the sweater that covered her shoulders like a cape. She tried to do up a button, but her arms were imprisoned by the sweater and she couldn't. Pierre put out his hand and helped her.

"I'll find a dog," he said. "And a cat. For you."

"Where?"

"There are farms on the road to the village. I've seen puppies, and kittens as well. They were lost."

"And you didn't keep them?"

"No."

"That's terrible! You left them to starve? And die of cold?"

"Yes. I was bad."

"That's not the point. But if you see any more, I hope you'll take them in and feed them and everything."

"And if you come back in spring, there they'll be. Nice ones, for you. I could ask the policeman, too. He kills lost dogs. And cats."

"Doesn't surprise me. But you be careful. Don't tell him anything. Don't tell him anything about me. Otherwise he'll stop me seeing you. He'll tell everything just to be a smart aleck and then they'll stop me. Understand?"

"When he came the other day I didn't say anything."

"He came back?"

"Yes. For a sturgeon."

"To nose around, more likely. And?"

"'Has the kid been here often?' That's what he said. I said: 'What kid?' 'Don't play innocent. That orphan kid.'"

"I hate him," Marie said fiercely.

"But he said he liked you. 'I wouldn't mind having her myself.' That's what he said."

"Oh."

"The sturgeon have been shy this year. I haven't seen one. But I had two plaice, two good ones."

"Did he take them?"

"'I'll give them to you.' That's what I said. And that was that. He didn't speak about you again. And I put the books under my bed. He didn't see a thing."

"So," said Marie. "Well, you're a cunning one!"

"And I'll tell him the dogs and cats are for me."

"Fine."

"A whole winter is long," said Pierre.

He looked at Marie, who didn't answer. He saw confusion in her eyes; they turned away. And Marie's lips were tight, very thin, tiny: she was pursing them the way a raccoon does when it swallows its food by the stream. Pierre wondered if Marie was thinking of crying?

After a moment's silence, Pierre said:

"If you like, I'll tell you about the caiplin." Still she did not answer. But she did look at him. He went on: "It happens every spring. When you'll be coming back."

"What is it?" said Marie.

"It's a fish, a young cod. The ice melts away from the beach and the mud flats, and the tide comes in over them very fast. Then the fish come to look. They're very fast. They're happy as can be, they go crazy. They dart in and throw themselves onto the land: they all leap out of the water together and flop everywhere—on the rocks, on the beach. They flop around all over the place; some fall back into the water, but you can pick up all you want on dry land.

That's the caiplin. At caiplin time everything begins again."

"Poor fish," said Marie.

"It's because they're happy. It's spring."

"A whole winter is a long time," said Marie.

Later that day, just before they said goodbye, Marie told him: "I'll bring you all the books I have. I'll start tomorrow. I'll put three or four in my bag, no one'll be any the wiser. I'll do it every day."

"They'll notice," said Pierre.

"Don't worry, I'll be careful. Maybe he'll think she threw them away. Maybe I'll leave a few. I'll fix it, don't worry." And Marie left him with a big wave of her hand. Then she blew him a kiss. He turned and went back over the rocks toward the path under the pines. Near a half-buried tree stump, he spotted a cache that smelled of fox fur. Yes, it'll soon be fall.

Pierre sat down with his back to the rock by the cabin and looked at the gulf.

The sun was sinking. On the horizon long, flat layers of cloud were piled on top of each other in close-packed strata, ablaze with every shade of orange and red. Out at sea the water was turquoise; at Pierre's feet it was almost black. . . . He dreamed, he spoke out loud, he smiled to himself. "I can read. And I know Marie. Before her, I knew nobody. All the other people I met were like the voices on the radio: strangers. But Marie! How could I have spent all that time, all those years, without even knowing that she was alive somewhere, with them? I just didn't know."

And now: "I'll come back." That's what she had

said. A bear cub turns over stones to get at the ants underneath. When he's finished he puts the stone back, so that the ants will return. Next year?

Then the sun began a sudden slide behind the clouds. It would be fine tomorrow, thought Pierre. The white gulls hovering in the sky were stained pink.

13

It was late afternoon. The sun sank, the tall pines assumed a solider bulk, their shadows lengthening across the dried grass and thorny shrubs. Withered raspberry bushes, leaves raining gold on the grass, slowly turned brown, then melted altogether into the dusk. Butterflies folded their wings in the hollows of shrubs whose own flowers were drooping and folding shut. These days, the wind dropped early if the tide was still out, and everything seemed to stand still to allow the day to take its leave in peace. If the tide was in, the *nordet* buffeted and bent the aspen and made the big pines creak and groan like a painful throat being cleared. It sent serried ranks of waves crashing against the shoreline where hazels bowed their heads at each lash. Crows and gulls rose like spray from the undergrowth by the shore, scattering and then flapping down again, ceaselessly harried by the turbulence of the gulf. When the wind finally dropped, earth and forest around the bay smelled of the sea, a smell of open, cloud-swept water.

Then vast stretches of forest stopped stirring and became patches of night, hanging across the distant mountains that were already dissolving into dark blues and violets. The western sky glowed pearl-gray. Stars blinked into view one by one in the north. In the east night was already smoldering.

The silence lasted an hour, and everything disappeared from sight. Then things began to emerge again, ghostly of shape and intricate of outline. From his bed Pierre listened to the undergrowth around the cabin. It was all familiar: for a long time the animals would wait, in holes in trees, at the mouths of their lairs, beside wide paths and narrow, twisting runs, along the lip of the beaver stream, under fallen rocks and in patches of fern. They would wait until everything was sure, given over to known dangers that would take their predictable course, given over to new discoveries and brief pleasures.

Beyond the expectant forest the *savane,* choked with thorns and tall grass, breathed with the gentle rhythm of night beneath the milky light of the moon and the noiseless flight of the brown owl. And beyond that wasteland of rustlings and furtive shadows, the hump of the Cape stood solid under its thick crown of pines, thrusting like a long, broad blade toward the open sea and the distant lights and beacons of the Iles. Down that huge, black prow, with its thin sprinkling of lights, the gravel road shone softly in the moonlight as it dipped gently down to the *savane.*

On the road Marie stopped running and looked at the night.

She had probably run all the way without stopping, all the way from the burning white house to the edge of the forest. Now the *savane* lay ahead. She had certainly run that far, run until she couldn't run anymore, until she reached the open sky. She was panting.

She listened. It seemed to her that she could still hear the crackling of flames. The smell of smoke was with her, on her, on her clothes perhaps. She breathed more easily; slowly her chest stopped heaving. She had the feeling that a thorn had gashed the back of her hand. She rubbed it in the dark.

Her legs began to move again without any conscious effort on her part. She took the path that sliced clumsily across the swampland, winding uncertainly among clumps of hemlock and wormwood, past sumac bushes and an occasional scraggy pine. You could see here. Marie looked up. The sky was milky from the light of an immense aurora and a moon as full as a dirty snowball. Marie felt very hot now. She stopped, took off her robe, threw it across her shoulders like a thick, twisted muffler, and went on. Her pajamas stuck on her chest and thighs. She broke into a trot, then slowed down again. Finally she fell into a less tiring step which gave her time to peer at the uncertain path ahead. Pierre's cabin was still far away.

Marie took her bearings from lone pines that thrust their bristling trunks above the clumps of undergrowth and brambles. She knew, more or less, in what direction she should expect to see the dark mass of the forest that led to Pierre. That way, eastward and a little to the left, after the mud flats whose iodine and damp grass she could already smell. She walked quickly, and soon she was near the trees. She felt confident as she walked along this semblance of a path so often trodden by Pierre, and perhaps by others. And there was the wood, just where she had been expecting it! Pierre's wood: all she had to do was cross it, and she would be at the cabin.

They're both dead, she thought suddenly, knocked senseless or suffocated. But they had already been senseless when she had gone to bed. The thought left her as abruptly as it had come, and she peered among the lower branches for the opening into the forest. After that, you just followed in Pierre's footsteps— along the grassy path, wide among the maple, aspen, and the big silver birch trunks that striped the darkness. The silence of the night was solid and black, like this stretch of forest. Not a rustle, not an animal call.

Marie walked very slowly at first, taking great care. She hesitated between two openings in the trees, examined them, found the way again, and walked on. Suddenly she was cold. She stopped, put her robe back on, and knotted the cord at her waist. Her eyes were getting used to the dark: now she could see pale rivulets of sand on the ground where the grass grew thin, clearly marking the path toward the cabin. She went on.

A crow clattered out of a pine with two sharp squawks and a loud flapping of wings. Marie smiled, as if at a good omen, a sign that she was indeed far from the Cape and would soon reach water and the open sky. The smell of smoke on Marie had dissolved in the cool air; the smell of fire hadn't reached this far; not yet, anyway. Nor fear either, perhaps. The maples were beginning to thin. Suddenly Marie realized she could hear the slap and fall of waves; the bay must be near. If you looked up, you could find your way by the dim light of the sky: the trees stood out against it, you just had to make for the widest opening, and there would be the water, first, then the rocks, then the cabin.

She no longer felt tired. Her steps, like her breathing, were steady. The forest opened in front of her. There was the house, with its heavy roof and low log walls. She shouted: "Pierre!"

"*Pierre!*" He thought he had heard Marie's voice. She was looking at him and laughing. Pierre opened his eyes, and smiled at his dream. One time she had asked, "What do you dream of when you sleep? I always dream, every night," she had added. He remembered now: he had dreamed that he and Marie were eating shrimp by the stove. They were wrapped in the sealskins his mother Nod had sewed together to make covers. They were warm, and afterward Marie gave him a sandwich of white bread and ham.

"Pierre, it's me, Marie!" He jumped quickly out of bed and opened the door. There she was in the moonlight. He took several steps into the night.

"The white house is burning! It's me, Pierre! Everything's burning up there!"

"You came here? At night? Is it you?"

"Of course, what do you think?"

He touched her shoulder; she pressed a little closer to him; she took his arm and shook it. "Come on!" she said. "We have to go up there." He woke up suddenly.

With one sharp, swift glance he took everything in: the forest, the rocks, the sky, the hour of the night, Marie wearing her robe, her face, her hands, the canvas sneakers on her feet. He dashed into the cabin and put on his coat and shoes.

She stood on the threshold, peering inside. "Wait a minute," she said. "Let me look." He found matches, lit a candle, and Marie came in. She walked all round the room and looked into the space next door where he stored his supplies. He watched her as she moved slowly around: she fingered one object after another in the half light of approaching dawn and the feeble glow of the candle. She leaned against the wall and stroked it with her hand. "Your house is beautiful," she said. "I'll remember it all. We have to go now. The police are there, and the neighbors, and those idiot firemen. They all saw me, they'll be looking for me all over. Come on."

Pierre walked ahead. Whenever the path between the trees narrowed he turned round to make sure Marie was following. As soon as there was room she caught up and trotted beside him.

"Yes, I can smell the smoke from here," he said. "A good wind to reach this far."

"I was reading in my room," said Marie, "before going to sleep. Luckily, right? When I put out the light I dreamed of what I'd been reading, the adventures of Don Quixote. I like Sancho, I was thinking of him, he's so funny. So naturally I was only half asleep when the smoke woke me up completely. . . . It was coming in through the door, everywhere, and on the other side there was this terrible crackling! I was

144

frightened, I put on my robe and tennis shoes as quickly as I could and got out through the window. What a sight! I just stood there, looking." She half-ran a couple of steps to keep up with Pierre.

"Then the neighbors came and there was a lot of yelling," she continued. "Like lunatics! You couldn't get into the house, there was too much smoke, it was all black, and it was blazing! Someone must've called the village, because the police and firemen arrived. Everyone was asking me things at once: 'Where are they? Are they inside? How did it happen? She got out through the window. In any case, we don't have any water! Are you cold? She's cold.' Naturally I was cold! And I was shivering because I was scared, wouldn't you? 'Cut boughs, we have to protect the wood! It might spread! Stand clear! Stand clear!' (That was the police, there were two of them.)"

"Look out," said Pierre. "There's a spring there, you'll have to jump." He was taking a shortcut across the *savane* that Marie didn't know. She was just following. She jumped, and grabbed his coat.

"They were so excited," she said, "that I sneaked away while they were running around. I walked slowly, and when I got to the road I ran. Before things got too complicated. I was thinking of you. I had to see you."

Now the smell alone could have told them of the scale of the disaster. And another smell mingled with the bitterness of the smoke—the damp fragrance of the herb that the people of Bas-du-Fleuve call *foin d'odeur,* the hemp that Pierre's mother Nod sometimes smoked and whose aroma now reached out to Pierre from the depths of his childhood. Then the sweet smell was gone, leaving nothing but the dirty reek of charred wood. They reached the edge of the swampland. Once they were on the road, treading the gravel, they were guided by the light—by the sky purple with fire in the distance behind the skeletal spruce tops.

A car was coming, from behind, from the village. They leaped into the ditch to avoid being seen, and it went past. They climbed back up on the shoulder and continued to walk. The fire appeared through the trees. The flames were already at ground level, and dying. Crackling, and voices. The sound of rhythmical blows, doubtless from the firefighters' branches. Without consulting each other, they moved a little way into the undergrowth. No one saw them arrive. They stopped a few steps behind a group of neighbors who were gaping at the disaster.

"I can't stay with you, Pierre," Marie whispered to him. "You understand why? They all saw me outside. How dumb! I should've run to our hideout near the water right away, or else under the trees to your place, without saying anything. They would've thought I was dead. That would've been fantastic: but they saw me. They were all saying, 'The girl wasn't burned, it's a miracle.' So if I disappear, they'll look everywhere for me. And the first place the police will look will be your house. Bam, prison, like that oaf said. And they'll take me back to the city in any case."

"Where to?" Pierre asked, his voice low.

"Hah! That I don't know, but I know what they'll do. They have convents, boarding schools, orphanages. . . . No worse than being with them. In fact, I think I'll be happy: in the orphanage they don't have time to bother anyone. Don't worry, I'll be all right."

"What about me?"

"Shh! You know everything you need to know to carry on and become a most learned man! I promise you! Look at that oaf: it's the old sea captain, he's trying to get near the fire, he'll go up in flames if he isn't careful. . . .

"There's the policeman pushing him back," she went on. "What are they all waiting for? What's the use of being firemen and putting on helmets and oilskins and everything? . . . How stupid! All they've managed to do is beat the bushes with bits of branch. Firemen without water! They could've hooked their hose up to the house next door. But no! Their pumps wouldn't have been powerful enough."

Pierre looked at Marie. She was crying. She was stifling the sobs between her nose and her throat, and you could hardly hear them, but her shoulders and chest rose and fell. She wiped her eyes with her hand, smiled, and said miserably to Pierre: "What's there to cry about? It's silly, I know. They're both in there. They didn't feel a thing. . . . They were drunk. They were bad, and here I am crying."

Pierre said nothing. He wanted to hold Marie's hand but was afraid to. After a while she said, "I remember when I was sick she gave me some fruit juice with medicine in it. That was the time she was so nice. When I was sick I thought I loved her. I felt so good, Pierre."

"Don't cry," he said. "Please stop. When you cry I get nervous, I don't know what to do."

"I've finished," said Marie, and cleared her throat. People turned and saw them. They came over. A woman said, "Poor little thing! She's an orphan now. . . . Sergeant!" she shouted. "Here she is."

The policeman came up and said, "So there you are! Where did you get to? Okay, listen, you come along with me now. No point in staying around till the end. There won't be anything to see. Are you cold?"

"Where are we going?" said Marie. "Just to see."

"Uh, well, I'll take you down to the village, to the bay, and you can spend the night with someone. I'm going to request instructions. Tomorrow we'll think about getting you back to the city, getting you home."

"Home is with them. There won't be anyone there."

"Poor little thing," said the woman.

"Well, listen, we'll see," said the policeman. "But just for now you come along, get in the car, you must be cold. And don't worry. . . . Hello," he said, turning round, "you here too, Le Rouge? Well, that makes everyone, I guess. Go and give them a hand." He shouted to the firemen and youths working round the huge, glowing pile: "Hey, get those two bodies out as quickly as you can! Get cracking, I'll be back with help. You," he said to the young policeman who had walked up, "stay here till I get back."

Marie hugged Pierre. She lifted her face and kissed him. Then, with her mouth to his ear, she said, "I'll come back. But don't ever tell anyone anything. Ever, ever, ever!"

"Come on, kid," said the policeman.

Next day and in the days that followed it went on getting colder. The *nordet* sent the aspen leaves whirling along the ground. The black pines groaned in every fiber, their tops swaying in the gusts high above.

From the *savane* came a variety of smells: the sharp tang of withered wild onion and the heavy odor of crowfoot, borne to the cabin in the cool of evening by the humid air of the flats.

Then there were endless, weeping rains that spilled the sound of the sleeping sea over the whole country. There were squalls, and curtains of heavy drops fell, then moved away. A distant flickering from a storm over the gulf illuminated the pale branches. Thunder rumbled softly and indistinctly. As night fell, a pinkish light flooded the bay. Next day the surface of the sea was restless; there were no waves, but a feeble swell washed long strands of kelp in among the gulls and ducks.

Pierre looks out at the gulf.

A killer whale, far off course, hurries to catch the outgoing tides, his black back sending up high waves as he slices through the troughs to open waters. Around him porpoise scatter, then re-form and follow in his wake. They're not afraid, not porpoises.

Borne on the wind, a flock of bustard wings steadily southward in a long V-formation. *Where is Marie?*

Here, where the North American continent ends, on the edge of the northern waters that lie between Pierre and his mother Nod's land, the land that never ends, the Baie-des-Epaulards will slowly fall silent again. And suddenly there will be nobody but Pierre, and everything will again be as it is.

The forests are already losing their leaves. Soon they will be no more than straight, stark, bare trunks rising from rusty ferns, dead leaves, and patches of early snow. The lightest footfall will crackle on the forest floor and will be echoed by a chorus of birds. Sometimes you hear the heavier tread of a deer or a moose. From a distance, Pierre will watch the moose walk down to the bank of the stream. It stops to drink. It looks cautiously all around, it listens. Then it crosses, the swift current foaming about its chest.

In the evening, winds. A prolonged high sound, amplified by sudden noisy gusts, shrilling endlessly and relentlessly through the bare branches.

On fall nights you hear coyote howling. And the furtive movements of marten and weasel just before they hole up to sleep or to keep warm. *Where will you be, Marie?*

150

Then the ice. The gulf packed with floes that invade the mud flats, then retreat and wedge themselves among the sleet-whitened rocks. It will snow for days, for a week, and the wind will begin to whistle again. Then there will be pack ice everywhere, and slush. Deep crevasses full of blue-green water and dead trees ferried out by the sea. Tides that go on for ever: that slide under the ice and lift it; it cracks, you can hear it all night, while the hungry gulls scratch through the empty petrel rookeries. And the wind, the wind that whips the powder snow in every direction; that flays every solid obstacle in your path—shattered tree trunks, rocks, boulders of living ice—and whirls the powder snow onward again. Then it will die and snow will fall cushioningly for another week. It will leap back to life and assault the snow again; it will whirl it and winnow it and stretch it out into long spiraling streams; it will weep and rage all night. And at daybreak the tide will go out, retreating beneath the floes, and the ice sheets will grow soft and subside, sinking slowly, revolving and colliding as they swim out on the current. Here and there the gulf will freeze hard—at estuary mouths, around islets where beacons and lighthouses flash—for a few hours or a few days. It will soon begin to move again, no one knows when.

Harp seal, bearded seal, grays, the big sea cows, every kind of seal will leave the water and bask on the floes. They will bark and flop around, they will slither and scratch in the sun and fill themselves with food. Pierre will make a hole in the ice and catch as many as he needs with his hook and line.

Pierre dreams. He had told Marie, "One year the

wolves crossed. They came from the far shore, I'm certain. They went past the cabin, I saw their tracks, there were seven of them. I can get across, too. Not often."

Pierre dreams. If he makes the crossing, maybe he'll go after mink and otter on the Iles, like his father. "Marie," he whispered out loud, "don't watch me hunt. Let me." The Iles-aux-Ours will be white, but underneath, under the roof of snow, it will be green. There'll be marten, Arctic hare, and the smell of rotting leaves. "You won't be there, Marie," he whispers again, "don't watch me. The gulls nesting on the cliffs will rise angrily as I come near."

Pierre dreams. Perhaps he won't go. If he finds a mink still alive in a trap one morning, not completely strangled, he'll take him in his hands very carefully and release him. Perhaps... he'll dart under the snow crust that covers last year's dead vegetation. Because Marie had said, "A live mink is so beautiful. I saw two in a cage once, it was disgusting. So." She always said, "So." The wounded mink won't last long; maybe a glutton will finish him off. Far from her eyes, far from Marie's eyes.

With the end of his stick Pierre will write the name "MARIE" on the snow, in the sun. On the snow of the Iles, the snow of the gulf, the snow of the forests. And in the pages of his notebook, in well-formed letters. Often, as he remembers what she had said, he will think of writing her name. Then, when he reads it, it will be as if Marie was with him in the cabin. Or outside, in the snow.

He will go into the woods in the morning. Down to the frozen stream. Out to the white dunes of the *savane,* the closed, forbidding *savane.* Down to the beach where the campers lived in summer. He will inspect his winter kingdom. Winter will shrink it slowly until March; then it will slowly grow again. Then he will hear a voice and the sound of a truck: it will be the Voyageur's first call of the year.

Maybe he'll find beaver holes in the ice. They smell of the lodges beneath, the smell of hot fur and feces. He'll find squirrel and marten holes. He will not want to disturb them: he will not know why. He knows he has to read a lot to know what Marie knows; he'll buy more books from the Voyaguer.

He'll learn why he is here and what he is doing here; he'll understand everything; and he'll think of Marie, too, Marie who has gone and who'll come back in some years, just when the sand irises are blooming blue at the foot of the water barley. He'll watch for the first flowers at the ends of the first stems, pointed, their petals still rolled tight, slowly turning blue. And he'll know why Marie was crying.

He'll think of Marie, and of how good it would be if she were here. He would see her every day; she might be angry, she might be smiling; she would be with him, and she would see everything he did. He would take her to the Iles if she wanted, and even to the far shore, the land that never ends. She wouldn't be afraid; she'd wanted to go there. He would hold her hand until the day the ice gave under their feet. But he would hold Marie's hand.

He'll wait. Marie had said that too, once. Pierre will try in vain to remember when. He will surely remember one day, while he is sawing wood, or making something, or eating. Or while he is reading one of her books, or the dictionary. He'll be able to read everything. He can read; quite fast, too; faster every day, understanding better every day how the words are connected to each other, in sentences that say what they say but say more: you hear something more in them than their voices, just like when Marie was talking and he was listening.

He can write now. That is, he knows the movements, all the movements, to make words speak on paper. Writing is slow, much slower than reading, but it, too, will come faster every day; and by changing the position of the words he will change the meaning of the words. What is writing for? He doesn't know, but it is for something: books are written. What is reading for? He doesn't know; he'll read the newspaper articles his father kept in that envelope. He'll learn his father's name; he'll learn who he was: a murderer.

Now there'll be no more surprises. He'll go into the damp shadows under the maples. There'll be tracks everywhere. When winter slows down and gets tired and waits for the first warm breezes that vanish as quickly as fleeting memories, he'll practice writing. One day, by the sweet smell of hazel shoots, he'll know the Cape has woken up. As he comes near he'll hear voices. He'll go along the road, and there'll already be someone in the house with the green shutters.

He'll walk toward the point of the Cape where the white house used to stand; just to see what the wormwood and moosewood have done to hide the ashes and the frost-twisted rubble.

Then he'll go to the clearing. There'll be letters on

a rock, his letters; and two other letters: her writing. With three legs. He'll smile.

He'll go to the hole under the spring. It'll need to be cleaned out. Then he'll come back home. He'll read, he'll erase, he'll write again; perhaps a book one day?

There's a step on the path; he hears it clearly. He gets up and opens the door.